"So, Anna," he began, his throaty voice
sending chills up her spine, **"how are
you doing?"**

To break contact with his compelling eyes, she
moved to the bench near the fountain and sat
down. She ran her fingers lightly through the cool
water, allowing her time to think of something
safe to say.

"I am doing much better, as you can see."

He came and sat next to her, sending all her good
intentions flying out of the garden. There was no
way she could look him in the eyes and keep her
composure, so she continued to watch her fingers
trailing through the water, smiling when a fish
came and began nibbling at them.

"It's amazing to me that you managed to travel
in the desert, in the dead of night, in such
a condition as I found you. You are truly a
remarkable woman."

Surprised, she finally looked at him and could see
that he was sincere. It pleased her that he regarded
her that way. At the same time, she wondered
exactly what was so notable about running away.
She doubted this man ran from anything.

DARLENE MINDRUP

is a full-time homemaker and homeschool teacher. Darlene lives in Arizona with her husband and two children. She believes romance is for everyone, not just the young and beautiful. She has a passion for historical research, which is obvious in her detailed historical novels about places time seems to have forgotten.

DARLENE MINDRUP

Love's Pardon

HEARTSONG
PRESENTS

Recycling programs
for this product may
not exist in your area.

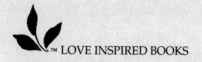 ™ LOVE INSPIRED BOOKS

ISBN-13: 978-0-373-48660-1

LOVE'S PARDON

Copyright © 2013 by Darlene Mindrup

www.LoveInspiredBooks.com

Printed in U.S.A.

A father to the fatherless, a defender of widows,
is God in His holy dwelling.
—Psalms 68:5

To my husband, my best friend.
I love you more than you will ever know.

Chapter 1

A full moon bathed the Palestinian landscape with light, lessening the stygian darkness of the warm spring night. Its round glowing orb reflected off the surface of the water rushing through the small wadi that wound its way through the countryside. The silence of the night was broken only by crickets chirping their cadences in sporadic communication.

A young woman knelt beside the flowing stream and plunged her shaking hands into its cool water, noting her distorted image reflected in its rippling surface. Blood was still seeping from the cuts on her face, purpling bruises marring what had never been beautiful features. She shivered at the face staring back at her. One eye was already swelling shut, her lips swollen and bruised. The blood from her cuts and scrapes would draw more than one predator, and she trembled at the moving brush around her. Lions were known to roam through this region of Judea.

Gathering her torn robe tightly around her, she curled up next to a large rock, trying not to imagine what might be lurking beneath its stony bottom. She shivered as the cool night air blew gently across her wet skin. Sighing, she leaned her head back against the boulder, allowing her thoughts to wander. Inevitably they turned to her father. Their last conversation still echoed in her mind.

"You will do as you are told!"

Anna had trembled at the look of raw fury in her father's eyes, but she knew that she couldn't give in. Not this time. The marriage he had arranged for her would be no better than trading one life of abuse for another.

"Please, Father. I can't," she pleaded, flinching from the blow she saw coming.

The first blow sent her head spinning, blood spurting from her mouth.

"The arrangements have already been made," he told her coldly. "You will marry Eli Barjonah in one week."

He stood waiting for her to agree. She should do so and avoid the beating she knew was coming, but something inside had finally snapped and she would give in no more. Let him do his worst; she didn't care any longer. Death was preferable to the life she had been leading for the last eighteen years since her mother's death. Let him kill her if he so desired. Better that than a life of fear and heartache. She had had enough of that to last her twenty lifetimes.

She was uncertain what caused her father to hate her so, but hate her he did. She could see it in the dark recesses of his eyes. He seemed to take great pleasure in finding fault with her, allowing him the opportunity to cause her physical pain.

Even though Eli Barjonah was known by all to be a hateful, brutal man, it seemed her father was pleased to be giving her over to him. Two of a kind, both full of malice and evil. What had she ever done to make him hate her so?

"I will not marry Eli, and you cannot make me." Defiance rang clearly in her voice.

Never having been pretty, she had reached twenty-five years of age without anyone ever having offered for her hand. Having no looks was one thing, but having no dowry, as well, had made her undesirable to the few men who might have been willing to overlook her plain appearance. Her father's frustration had grown with each passing year. Had her mother lived, things might have been different, but life was what it was.

For years she had tried to please her irascible father, all to no avail. No matter what she did, she was always wrong in his eyes. How had her mother endured such a man? The circumstances of her death were still a mystery to Anna, but she had her suspicions. Oh, yes. She had her suspicions. And it was those very suspicions that had sent her fleeing into the night regardless of what might be lurking in the darkness, regardless of who might be lurking in the darkness. Only her complete faith in Elohim had given her the courage to make such a move. Had He not sent His only Son to die for her? Such a Father she could love and honor, a Father unlike any she had ever known. It still filled her with awe that He would allow His Son to die for such a one as she. What was even more remarkable was the fact that He had died for her father, as well. Incredible!

Thankfully her father hadn't known of her conversion to the Way or she knew for certain that she wouldn't be alive today. She believed it would have given him great pleasure to see her stoned to death for forsaking her Jewish beliefs. But she hadn't really. Jesus was actually the fulfillment of the Jewish faith. If only more people could understand that.

An owl hooted in the distance, bringing her thoughts

back to the matter at hand. She should get moving, but the pain in her side had become more intense as she walked over the rough terrain. It was so hard to breathe. More than likely, her father's last beating had broken a few ribs.

She tried taking a deep breath, but the lancing pain that shot through her chest sent a dizzying wave through her that almost made her pass out. Tears started from dark brown pain-filled eyes as she lifted them heavenward.

"Elohim! Help me!" Her voice was a bare sigh escaping upward on the night wind.

Regardless of the pain, she had to get moving again. She wasn't far enough away from her father's reach. Her defiance of him would not let him rest until she finally subjected herself to his will. He was that kind of man.

She attempted to rise, but the effort was too much. Whimpering in pain, she lay prostrate on the cold sand and, forgetting the faith she had just advocated, she begged for a quick death.

She lay weeping for some time before she realized that something was tickling her hand. Without moving her body, she slowly lifted her face and peered through the darkness. The large black creature crawling across her hand made her forget everything—broken ribs, pain, cuts and bruises. With a scream that resounded around the surrounding hillsides, she flung the scorpion into the night.

Lucius Tindarium reclined on the hard, sandy ground beside the fire, relaxing for the first time in days. He brushed back dark hair that had been blown across his forehead by the gentle night breeze. His men were scattered around him, some fast asleep, others deep in conversation. The sheen from their helmets and gear reflected the light from various fires. One guard stood watch just beyond the perimeter of light.

It had been a long, grueling month of working on the roads that Rome had a reputation for building, and they were finally heading back to the Antonia Fortress in Jerusalem. All along this particular section of road, thieves and cutthroats hid among the rocks and ravines looking for helpless victims. He pitied any man, or men for that matter, who would be foolish enough to attack his group. Few they might be, but they made up for their small numbers with their excellent fighting ability.

Stars shimmered in the dark night sky, and he watched, fascinated, as one streaked to earth. A good omen, or so the priests said. Perhaps he would finally be recalled to Rome and he could leave this desolate region with its stubborn, warring people.

His lips tilted wryly. Then again, were his people any better? Twenty years he had served in Rome's legions. Twenty years of fighting and killing. His service was required for twenty-five years. In five years he could retire. But would he?

He lay back, folding his arms beneath his head and continuing to study the stars above him. Was his destiny truly tied to those small flashing bits of light? Would they give him the answers to the questions he wasn't even able to put into words?

Scars all over his hard, lean body spoke of his life as one of Rome's finest warriors. He had advanced to the rank of tribune at a young age, his keen insight and fierce fighting style having helped to win many a battle. He knew without conceit that his men would blindly follow him into whatever area he chose to go, into death if necessary. Their devotion to him was absolute.

The scream that pierced the still night air made the hair on his neck stand on end. Both he and his men who were awake were on their feet instantly, swords drawn.

Those who had been sleeping scrambled for their weapons, searching the darkness for what had invaded their sleep-weary minds.

"It came from over there, Tribune."

Lucius's look followed the man's pointing finger, but he could see nothing in the moon-bathed landscape. Andronicus and Hermes, his bodyguards, stood on each side of him, the intent look on their faces causing Lucius to smile. The same deadly look filled his own eyes.

"Could it have been a lion?" Andronicus asked, his voice pitched low.

Lucius stood in indecision. Should he seek out the source of the scream and possibly fall into an ambush, or stay here and wait? Here they had the advantage. Out there, they could be easy targets.

"It sounded like a woman," Hermes stated quietly.

"What would a woman possibly be doing out here?" Andronicus questioned.

"You're asking me? What are *we* doing out here? What would anybody be doing out here in this wretched place?"

Lucius silenced his diatribe with a glare and made his decision. "Well, let's go and find out. Someone might need our help."

Hermes and Andronicus shared a look that Lucius had no problem interpreting. It would not bode well for whoever had interrupted their rest. He hid a grin.

"Callus, you and the others stay here and guard the equipment. I'll take Hermes and Andronicus with me."

"Aye, Tribune." The guard looked less than satisfied with his orders.

Hermes lit a torch from the fire, and Lucius and Andronicus followed him as he slowly edged his way toward the place where the sound had originated. Their hobnailed boots clicked against the rocks scattered throughout the area.

Every muscle in Lucius's well-toned body was tense with anticipation, his sword clutched tightly in his fist. His eyes scanned the surrounding landscape looking for any sign of movement.

Before long, they arrived at the bank of the wadi. They had camped here for the very reason that it was flowing with water, of which they had made full use. Rocks and bushes made shadows against the moonlit sand, giving the illusion of enemies where there were none.

It was because his look was outward that Lucius missed the object lying at his feet. He stumbled over it, grabbing Andronicus to keep from pitching forward. Both men straightened themselves, glancing at their feet.

Andronicus sucked in a breath. "It's a woman!"

Kneeling quickly, Lucius carefully turned the woman over, flinching when he saw her bruised face. She was small and slim and he wondered how someone so slight could endure such a beating. Questions sprang to his mind in rapid succession, the one registering uppermost being whether she was a runaway slave.

Andronicus knelt beside him, his look quickly gliding over the woman. "Is she alive?"

The question succeeded in bringing Lucius quickly back to the moment at hand. He felt for a pulse and was reassured by a faint but steady rhythm. He moved his hands quickly over the rest of her body. If she had other injuries, he couldn't tell without first unclothing her, and he couldn't do that here in the faint light from the torch.

"She's alive, but barely. Get Antigonus."

Andronicus left to get the acting physician of their troop. Lucius couldn't take his eyes from the seriously marred face. It was hard to put an age to the young woman, so badly was she disfigured. He had seen a lot of things in his time, even women more disfigured than this, but something about this one penetrated to a heart he had thought long inured to such sights, and he couldn't for the life of him explain why.

Hermes knelt beside him. "She looks to be Jewish from her clothing. Do you think she's a runaway?"

Lucius could tell she was running away, but from what? Or more precisely, from whom? He was kept from answering by the arrival of Antigonus. Kneeling beside Lucius, the surgeon's lips compressed into a tight line. A soldier of Rome he might be, but he had a sister and such sights never failed to anger the younger man.

Antigonus pointed out the bruises on the woman's arms. "If I were to hazard a guess, I would bet that she has more marks on other parts of her body." He shook his head. "I'm afraid to move her without being able to see the extent of her injuries."

"Well, we can't leave her here," Lucius disagreed. Fingers gliding across her forehead, he gently pushed the hair from her face. He turned to Hermes. "Make up a litter. We'll just have to take as much care as possible."

Antigonus glanced speculatively from Lucius to the woman. "She's still unconscious. That will make it easier on her, but harder for us to know just how much damage we might be inflicting."

"She can't have been unconscious long," Lucius told him. "It was her scream that brought us here."

"Whatever made her scream must have caused her to do something that sent her into unconsciousness."

"Or whoever," Lucius commented, his look once again scanning the surrounding terrain.

Hermes and Andronicus brought the litter and both Lucius and Antigonus gently lifted the woman onto it. She moaned slightly, but never awakened.

Lucius walked beside the litter on one side while Antigonus walked on the other. Although keeping an eye on the area around them, both men couldn't help but glance at the woman from time to time. Each man's thoughts were reflected on his face; none were pleasant.

When they reached the campsite, Lucius sent more men to guard the surrounding area. They settled the litter close to the fire and left to allow the young physician to attend the woman.

Lucius moved to a spot closer to the fire. He sat cross-legged, his arms draped between his legs, intently watching Antigonus as he worked over the woman. He would give his month's salt rations to know what had happened to her. His concern baffled him. What was there about this woman that had his thoughts so firmly fixed on her?

The other soldiers glanced their way periodically, but few were discomfited by the woman's condition. They had seen too much in their years to be bothered by one mutilated woman. It was hard to live the life of a soldier and not become immune to others' pain. So why was Lucius so disconcerted by this one woman and, from the robe she wore, a Jewess at that?

To be honest, he knew the answer to that. Looking at the girl was like looking at his own mother. He was himself half Jew. His mother lived in Jerusalem in the upper city where the wealthy resided, consort of a Roman soldier. At least she had been until his father was killed in a campaign in Germania.

Since it was forbidden for legionnaires to marry, his father and mother had lived together as man and wife. In their own eyes, they were married. Roman tolerance would allow such, but here in Palestine, his mother had been an outcast. Bad enough that she lived with a man without being married, but that man was a Roman, which made it twice a crime in Jewish eyes. Only the fact that she was under Roman protection had kept her from being accosted physically, though mental tribulation had been as hard for her to bear.

The Jews hadn't needed to punish her physically; his father had seen to that aspect of her life. Many a day Lucius had come home to find his mother with a face bruised by his father's hand. She always had an excuse, but he knew. Too often he had experienced his father's wrath himself.

When he was old enough, he had been sent to Rome to learn Roman ways. He had fought tooth and nail to stay with his mother, but his father had been adamant. Shortly after he had been sent away, his father had gone to Germania and been killed. In truth, he had been relieved to hear it. He had never understood why his mother had stayed with such an abusive man.

Seeing the woman across the way had brought back old feelings of anger and pain. Memories that had long been buried were suddenly brought into the light once more. Even if the girl was a slave and had been beaten by her master, the similarities were too striking to ignore. But what if she was escaping an abusive husband? It could cause complications that Roman leaders were trying to avoid.

A distant roar came from the darkness beyond their campsite.

Antigonus lifted himself from the woman's side and crossed to Lucius. Their eyes met.

"A lion," Antigonus suggested. "Probably following the woman's blood trail."

Lucius pressed his lips together into a grim line. "Where there is one, there are probably others, and other predators, as well."

Lucius motioned to the nearest soldier. "Take some men and gather more brush for the fire."

The soldier slapped his right fist against his chest. Lucius stopped him as he was about to turn away.

"And Democidus, bring the watches in closer to the fire. Make certain everyone understands the situation."

"Aye, Tribune."

Lucius once again returned his attention to Antigonus. "How is she?"

He shook his head. "Hard to say. Her irregular breathing tells me that she probably has fractured ribs. She is going to be incapacitated for quite some time." He squatted down, using the amphora of water sitting close by to wash his hands. "What will you do with her?"

"What can I do?" Lucius shrugged. "We can't very well leave her here. We'll reach Jerusalem tomorrow. I'll take her to my mother."

Antigonus met his look. "Someone is bound to be looking for her."

Lucius's chin settled into hard lines, but he said nothing. Antigonus wisely left the tribune to his thoughts.

Chapter 2

Lucius strode into his mother's home, the coolness of the surrounding marble and tile a relief from the oppressive Palestinian heat outside. Business had kept him from visiting his mother since he had dropped the mystery woman with her two days before, and he was anxious to find out how she had fared. The past two days had been filled with his duties, but his nights had been filled with dreams wherein the aforementioned woman had figured highly.

He handed his uniform cape to the servant waiting at the door and impatiently waved away her apparent intent to wash his sandaled feet. She placed the washbasin aside and waited for any further instructions.

"Where is my mother?"

"In the sick room, m'lord."

He hurriedly mounted the stairs to the upper balcony. Leah met him at the top of the stairs, a finger to her lips to silence him.

As usual, he marveled at his mother's delicate beauty even after almost six decades. Her gray hair was loosely knotted on top of her head, not a wayward tress out of place. Even after his father's death, she preferred keeping to the Roman style. It had always confused him that she would do so when it so marked her as a Roman and not a Jew. Had she returned to her Jewish roots, she no doubt would have had an easier time among the people of Jerusalem, but then again, she had never chosen an easy life. He glanced past her to the open door.

"How is she?"

At his mother's protracted sigh, Lucius knew the news would not be good.

"She's burning with fever," she told him worriedly. She took him by the arm and moved him toward the stairs again. "Let us go into the triclinium where we can talk in comfort."

He reluctantly allowed her to lead him down the stairs and into the area used for dining. The table was set and Lucius realized that his mother had been preparing to eat her noon meal.

"I'm interrupting your lunch." He started to pull back. "I can come back later."

"Nonsense," she argued. "You can join me. Are you hungry?"

Lucius realized that he was indeed famished. His stomach growled a protest at the fragrances drifting from the food on the table. His mother laughed.

"I thought as much." She grinned. "You need someone to take care of you."

He smiled wryly in return. His mother had been saying that for years. "That's what I have soldiers for," he told her, kissing her cheek. "And a mother."

Her soft laughter brought a faint smile to Lucius's face.

Motioning one of the servants to bring another plate, she then directed Lucius to the reclining couch across from hers.

The triclinium was one of his favorite rooms in this house. The wall murals of the Tiber River and its surrounding countryside always made him feel as though he was back in Rome, and he felt the tension slide from his body. No doubt the paintings were done at his father's instigation and probably had had the same effect on him.

Lucius waited until they were seated before resuming their conversation.

"The woman, you say she is burning with fever. How bad do you think it is? Do you think she will survive?"

It was something he had worried about for the past two days. For some reason, he just could not get the woman off his mind no matter how hard he tried. The thought of her dying left him feeling oddly depressed.

"She needs more help than I can give her," Leah told him, her soft voice an indicator of her feelings on the matter. It would seem that the mystery woman had affected her, as well.

The serving girl who had met him at the door placed a silver plate in front of him. He glanced up to thank her and met the sultry invitation in her eyes. It wasn't the first time this particular servant had shown interest in him. Unlike some men who would have been pleased with the inducement, he preferred to do his own hunting. Frowning, he turned away, his dismissal evident. The smile fled from her face and, turning her nose up, she flounced from the room.

Leah looked from one to the other before reaching for the sliced pheasant. It wasn't just a mother's pride that told her that her son was one of the finest specimens of manhood that Elohim had created. Like many soldiers of Rome, his physique was toned, the muscles evident even through the chest plate of his uniform. His face could easily have graced a Roman statue.

"So, that's the way it is."

Lucius didn't like the way his mother was smiling. "No, that's not the way it is," he refuted. "Believe me, I have never dallied with any of your servants."

He gave her a look that would have quelled one of his troops; it had no effect whatsoever on his mother.

"But not from lack of invitation, I suspect," she retorted.

Ignoring the statement, Lucius returned to the subject uppermost in his mind. "If you need help I will send for Phlegon."

His mother made a rude sound with her lips. "That old goat? I will not have him step foot in my house!"

Lucius was surprised at her vehemence. "He is one of Rome's finest physicians," he argued.

"If he is such a fine physician, then why is he here in Jerusalem instead of Rome? A man who uses insects to suck the life out of someone is one of Rome's finest? Rome can keep her finest then. No wonder Rome loses so many of her soldiers if they have physicians like that!"

Lucius frowned. Part of him agreed with what she said, but the more logical part of his mind, which realized that Phlegon had studied medicine under one of the wisest and most respected surgeons in the world, disagreed.

"Mother, if she has a fever, she needs to be bled."

The enigmatic look she threw him puzzled him, having never seen it before. It was mysterious, and that coming from his mother astounded him. She was one of the most honest and forthright people he had ever known, and there weren't many.

"The scriptures teach us that life is in the blood," she told him firmly, rolling a sliver of pheasant in a flat bread.

"If you remove the blood, you remove the life. It's as simple as that."

Surprised at her reference to the Hebrew writings, it took him a moment to decipher the direction of their conversation. He settled back against the cushions, one eyebrow winging upward.

"Ah. The scriptures." Many things about his mother had changed when she married a Roman, but rejecting the Jewish scriptures hadn't been one of them. Periodically she would throw out some tidbit of wisdom from the scriptures that usually left him flummoxed. He knew better than to argue because there would be no swaying her. It was obvious that she now had her mind set on a particular course of action. He decided to play the game her way.

"Well, Mother. What would you suggest then?"

The sunlight spilling in from the open doors to the balcony revealed lines in her face that he hadn't noticed before. Although still lovely, her age was definitely beginning to tell on her. Concern furrowed his brow.

She began pulling grapes from the cluster on the table and adding them to her plate.

"There is a Jewish rapha in Bethany. He would know what to do."

Lucius stared in surprise at this pronouncement. Bethany? That was at least six miles from Jerusalem.

"Are you by any chance suggesting that I go to Bethany and retrieve this…this rapha? And what is a rapha?"

She continued filling her plate. "A rapha is a healer. This one is old, but he has forgotten more about healing than your old Phlegon will ever know. The Jews have been ministers of healing for many ages."

Smiling wryly, Lucius shook his head. Where had this sudden desire to defend her people come from, especially when they had been so unkind to her? She was sounding more like a Jew every minute.

"Does this healer have a name?"

Recognizing the question for the capitulation it was, she gave him a smile that made the years disappear from her face. It left him strangely unsettled. His instincts told him that there was something more going on here than was apparent on the surface.

"His name is Levi. He lives on the outskirts of Bethany as you come into the village."

"And how on this earth do you happen to know that?"

In all the years he could remember, his mother had never traveled farther than the lower city in Jerusalem.

She quickly lowered her eyes to her plate and Lucius's suspicions grew.

"Remember, I am from Bethany."

That was certainly true, but it had been years since she had even mentioned it. He continued to study her, questions tumbling through his mind that he was reluctant to bring forth. He had a sudden foreshadowing of something about to happen that would change his world forever.

He opened his mouth to speak but was interrupted by a servant hurrying into the room.

"My lady, come quickly. The woman will do herself an injury!"

Both Lucius and his mother came to their feet, Lucius swiftly passing his mother and taking the steps two at a time. He made his way to the bed where the woman was thrashing wildly about. He sat on the side of the bed and pinned her by her arms, talking to her in a soothing tone of voice.

Her dark, matted hair spread across the pillow in wild abandon as she thrashed about. More bruises had darkened on her face and he ground his teeth together in anger.

She continued squirming, her head turning from side to side.

"No, Father! Please!"

Her husky, pleading voice settled coldly in his midsection. The word father tumbled through him like an avalanche of lava, bringing forth a dark anger that had simmered inside him for many a year. Her whimpering voice filled with terror sent a prism of pure rage through Lucius. He continued talking to her, trying to soothe her, but her thrashing only intensified.

His mother reached around him, placing her hand against the woman's forehead.

"She's still burning up with fever! Bring me some cool water."

The servant who had followed them into the room ran to do her bidding.

"Lucius, let me try. Your voice seems only to make matters worse."

Reluctantly, Lucius moved from the bed and allowed his mother to take his place. She pulled the woman up into her arms as she would an infant and began rocking her and humming a tune she had often used with him as a child.

Ever so slowly the Jewess relaxed in his mother's arms. Lucius met his mother's look and knew that she was remembering, as he was, the many times she had held him thus as a child after one of his father's beatings. As it had then, so now her singsong voice managed to calm the rage flowing through him.

"Go quickly, Lucius," she whispered. "Find Levi the healer and bring him here."

Lucius had his doubts about whether a Jew would enter the home of a Roman, but he was not beyond a threat or two if it came to that. He quickly left to do her bidding, his mind suddenly filled with images of his past.

* * *

Anna clawed her way through a cloying labyrinth of darkness. Unknown voices moved in and out of her consciousness, voices calling her to the light she could see through the obsidian depths.

At times a soft feminine voice brought a soothing calm to her. In her world of half wakefulness, she could believe her mother was still alive. Soft, gentle hands soothed her brow and brought forth the peace she had known years before.

One voice in particular, strong and vibrant, pulled at her, drawing her forth; a voice she somehow recognized. She could no more resist that voice than she could stop breathing, for to do either would mean certain death.

"Anna, come back to us," that voice commanded again and she tried harder to respond, but her eyelids were so heavy.

"She seems to be coming round."

That voice, too, was a familiar one, one that brought sudden fear to her heart.

Anna struggled against the darkness trying to suck her into oblivion. But, why? Would it not be better to let go and find that peace she had found in the darkness?

"Woman! Come back to the land of the living. Fight him. Do not give in to Pluto!"

Pluto? Was he not the supposed god of the Roman underworld? Why would she give in to some imagined god when she had the great God of the universe as her master?

"Open your eyes!"

The command in the voice succeeded in reaching past the fog in her mind. Dragging open her eyes, Anna saw through the semidarkness a face close to her own. She could make out no features, but it was a man she had never seen before. Surprised, she pushed back against the pillow that was cradling her head. The move made shock waves of pain thunder through her head.

"Where...where am I?" she groaned.

The dryness in her throat brought on a fit of coughing, pain racking her chest and adding to her already extreme discomfort.

"Bring me some water!"

Again, that commanding voice. Large, gentle hands lifted her head and a cup was placed against her lips. "Drink."

Gratefully, she did as she was told. She would have gulped the whole cup but he pulled it away.

"Easy. Not too much at one time."

The water had relieved some of the dryness in her throat and she sighed with relief. Her world was coming into focus once again. She began to take note of her surroundings.

She was in the most comfortable bed she had ever known. The texture of silk sheets slid against her skin. Soothing. Calming.

The room she was in was large, larger than her entire house. The walls were of plaster with frescoes adorning their surfaces. She couldn't make out the pictures in the dim lamplight. Where on Elohim's great earth was she? And for that matter, how did she get here?

Another man moved into position behind the one sitting beside her on the bed.

"Hello, Anna."

Levi. A cold prism of fear shivered through her. What was Levi doing here? And who was this other man?

A clean-shaven face told her he was no Jew. Her look wandered over his lean, muscular body. She recognized the uniform of Rome and her heart sank. What evil plan had her father instigated now that included a Roman?

She started to rise, but gasped as excruciating pain in

her side ripped through her. The Roman gently but firmly pushed her back against the bed. His brown eyes flashed fire.

"Be still, woman. Do you want to undo everything we've done for you?" he snapped in evident irritation.

"Where am I?" she asked again. Her voice was barely a whisper as she struggled to comprehend what was happening. Nothing here was familiar. What was she doing here? Panic began to swell through her.

Seeing her distress, the other man tried to calm her.

"You are in my mother's home. We found you in the desert. You were severely beaten. Do you remember anything?"

Murky images began to flash through her mind. She had been running away from her father's forced marriage. Her look of panic flew to Levi's face.

Levi knew her, and knew her well. Indeed, they came from the same village. Had he already told her father of her whereabouts? Levi's gentle smile almost succeeded in calming her. Almost.

"Tell me what happened, child," Levi asked.

If he hadn't already, Levi would tell her father where she was and she would be hauled back and forced into an abominable marriage with a man who was even more wicked than her own father.

"Does my father know where I am?" she asked, her fear evident.

Lucius looked from one to the other and suddenly the conversation he had had with the old healer made perfect sense.

When he had first brought the man here, he was surprised to find that Levi knew the woman. She was from Bethany, as was Levi. She hadn't traveled a great distance that night that now seemed so long ago, but in her condition it was amazing that she had gotten as far as she had.

It was Levi who had told him the woman's name, and he hadn't been surprised to see her in the condition she was in, though he refused to give Lucius any information other than her name. Now he knew why. Her fear of her father was palpable, which told Lucius who exactly was responsible for her condition. He had suspected as much.

Levi gently brushed the hair from her face, giving her a reassuring smile.

"No, Anna. I don't believe so."

She gave a relieved sigh. Brown eyes filled with trepidation settled on Lucius. "Who are you? Why am I here?"

"My name is Lucius. You are in my mother's home in the Upper City of Jerusalem."

Anna's eyes widened in alarm. The Upper City was where the wealthy lived, Jew and Gentile alike.

"How…?"

Lucius answered her unspoken question. "As I told you. My men and I found you in the desert. I didn't know what else to do, so I brought you to my mother."

Her gaze quickly scanned the room.

"No, she is not here right now…"

He was interrupted by a soft, feminine voice. "Yes, I am."

Lucius turned at his mother's voice, his smile freezing in place at the strange look on Levi's face. His mother and the old healer were staring at each other as though they were familiar with each other, Levi in obvious shock. Lucius opened his mouth to speak when his mother's next words silenced him in surprise.

"Hello, Father."

Chapter 3

Anna had no idea what was happening. The Roman, Lucius, sat frozen in shock as well as old Levi. The woman, who had to be Lucius's mother, moved with grace and assurance into the room, although that assurance was not reflected on her face.

She was uncommonly beautiful, her Roman dress flowing about her ankles as she crossed the room. The yellow color of the saffron-dyed material reflected in the white of her hair that just touched her temple. It was obvious that she was the only one who understood the drama playing out around them.

"Leah!"

Levi's voice was barely above a whisper. He shook his head slightly as though to chase away some figment of his imagination.

The Roman rose to his feet, his frowning look going from his mother to the old physician.

"What is this?"

Unlike Levi's, Lucius's voice thundered around the room.

Her own plight forgotten in the drama of the moment, Anna stared from one person to the other. She knew the story of the healer. His daughter had married a Gentile and had been cut off by her people. Unlike with *niddui* excommunication, she had the most severe *herem* pronounced against her, which excluded her from any Jewish gathering or association. Anna hadn't been born when that happened, but she knew that Levi mourned the loss of his only daughter. And the same thing would happen to her if her father ever found out that she had become a follower of the Way.

Leah stepped forward and, while silencing her son with an upraised hand, her look never wavered from Levi. They stared at each other for several seconds before Leah's attention turned to Anna.

"How are you, my dear? Are you feeling better?"

The men took their cue from her and turned to Anna, as well. She squirmed under their focused scrutiny. The Roman was looking at her as though she were to blame for the tension permeating the room.

"I...I..." What was she to say? How could she possibly answer that? The pain was still intense, so much so that it was hard to breathe, but at this moment, she would have given anything to be able to walk out of this house.

Levi spoke up. "It will be some time before she will be well. Her wounds are severe, as well as the broken ribs that I suspect."

Leah turned to him, seemingly surprised that he had even spoken to her. Sudden tears formed in her eyes.

"Perhaps we could speak in the triclinium," she suggested to him in a choked voice. Her edgy posture silently pleaded with him to agree.

Levi hesitated, but then jerked his head once in affirmation. Lucius's mouth tightened into a thin line at their silent exchange. He turned to follow them from the room when his mother's voice halted him.

"Please stay with Anna, Lucius. I prefer that she not be left alone."

Lucius opened his mouth to speak but snapped it shut at his mother's negative shake of the head. His lips tightened further, making him look so fierce that Anna felt her own heart start to thump with trepidation. She would hate to be the recipient of such a look. Yet, amazingly, he gave way and remained standing where he was.

He continued to stare at the door long after they had left the room. Anna felt as though she were in the middle of one of the Greek dramas the Hippodrome was so famous for.

Anna shifted position to relieve the pressure on her lower back, and Lucius turned to her with a look that suggested he had forgotten she was in the room. He lifted a brow in query and Anna wanted to sink through the cushions. He was certainly a formidable-looking man.

"I am sure that it would not harm me to be left alone," she told him encouragingly. The look he gave her spoke volumes and dropped her into silence. He chose to ignore her statement.

"Is there something I can get for you? Do for you?" he asked absently, his look once again focusing on the closed portal.

Not if her life depended on it would she admit to such. She shook her head slightly, knowing that too much movement would send excruciating waves of pain through her head and sides.

He ignored her attempt to relieve him of duty and poured her a glass of water anyway. The green glass goblet was beautiful, a specialty found only in Jerusalem. Lucius's mother must be wealthy indeed to afford such luxuries.

Lucius helped raise her slightly, wincing with her as she struggled against the pain. He held the glass to her lips, this time allowing her to get her fill of the thirst-slaking liquid.

She leaned back against the pillows, allowing her breath to slowly sigh from her in relief.

"Your father is responsible for this?"

Her eyes flew to his. There was a darkness in his gray eyes, giving them the look of molten silver, that sent a shiver of pure fear through her. How to answer that? And if she did would he then feel it his duty to return her to her father? Perhaps he was like most men and believed women to be nothing more than chattel.

As though he could read her thoughts, he told her softly, "Have no fear. I have no intention of returning you to your father."

Anna relaxed somewhat, but continued to watch him warily. What exactly did his plans entail then?

"Why did he do it? What great sin had you committed to deserve such a beating?"

What great sin indeed? Her only sin had been in wanting to live! Anna dropped her lashes, her fingers twisting nervously together in her lap. "I refused to marry the man he chose for me."

Lucius's eyebrows flew up in surprise. He wasn't quite sure what to say. He had assumed that the woman had done some minor infraction that an abusive father would have felt justified in meting punishment over. Refusing to marry, though, this was something much more serious. Marriages were arranged all the time among both Jew and Gentile. He had never heard of a woman refusing the partner her parents chose for her.

He felt sorry for the woman, but right now she was the least of his concerns. What he wanted more than anything at this moment was to march down the stairs, storm into the triclinium and demand an explanation. He had a grand-father! Why did his mother never tell him?

"You had a reason?" he asked the woman absently, catching her look.

Her soft brown eyes hardened into brown agate, her knuckles turning white where they clutched the silken sheets.

"He is an evil man!"

The intensity of her voice left him in no doubt of what she said. Surprisingly, he believed her. He wasn't quite certain what to say to such a scathing comment. He decided to let it pass.

"You will be safe here," he assured her, a slight smile briefly touching his lips.

For a moment, he lost himself in her liquid eyes. Tears shimmered across the surface, releasing one lone drop to slide slowly down her bruised cheek, and he wondered if she was in pain or if it was from some hurtful memory.

"I cannot stay here," she whispered.

Thinking he understood, his anger was aroused. It had always been thus whenever he thought that his mother was being slighted. The anger had been a part of him for so long he wasn't sure what he would be like without it.

"Because I am a Gentile? Or because my mother has been shunned by your people?"

She stared at him in shock. "Neither," she told him, her voice holding censure. "I cannot stay because my father is certain to find out where I am and come for me. I need to get as far away as possible."

His anger evaporated as quickly as it had come.

"You will be safe here," he assured her again. "I doubt even your father would think of looking for you in the house of a Roman."

"But if Levi tells him…"

"I will see that he does not," he interrupted her.

He wasn't exactly sure how he would arrange for the man's silence, but he would find a way even if it meant arresting the old man for some trumped-up charge. Still, his words did nothing to reduce her anxiety. He could hardly blame her, knowing the atrocities his people had committed against hers. But then, such atrocities went both ways. His friend Gallus had been killed by an assassin only two weeks ago.

Anna was staring at him as though he were a lion about to pounce. And then it dawned on him. She was afraid of *him*. He crossed the room, pulled the stool that was next to the bed closer and sat down next to her. Her eyes widened at the action, at least the one that wasn't swollen almost completely shut. What was there about those eyes? They were almost mesmerizing.

"Anna, you need have no fear of me. I will not harm you." His voice had grown husky and he cleared it, trying to infuse his look with some kind of assertion. He had a feeling he failed miserably. She didn't relax at his words. She studied him skeptically instead.

"I…I am not afraid of you."

He barked a laugh at this pronouncement, making her jump slightly. He returned her skeptical look in full measure. She truly wasn't much to look at, especially in her condition. Yet, there was something about her.

"Let us, for the sake of argument, say that I believe you," he quipped. "Perhaps it would help you to know that I am rarely at this house. It belongs to my mother and I visit with her as much as I am able, but my duties take me elsewhere most of the time."

Some of the tension eased from her, but her eyes still

held doubt. He couldn't think of a way to relieve her of her concern. She would just have to see for herself.

His mother entered the room and he jumped to his feet. He studied her face to see if there was any sign of stress. The tears were obvious and he felt his gut clench with anger. So help him, if her father had done anything to hurt her, he would see him hanging from a spear before the night was out. Instead, his mother's face shone with joy. Brows drawing together, he looked beyond her to Levi entering the room behind her and saw the same joy radiating from his features.

"Lucius, I need to speak with you in the peristyle. My father will stay with Anna."

"Please," Anna interrupted. "Do not concern yourself with me."

His mother merely lifted an eyebrow at him, motioning with her head. Lucius's narrow-eyed look made the rounds of those in the room. This situation was out of his control, something he had never dealt well with. He was used to being in command, yet he felt like a ship without a rudder against the onslaught of events surrounding him.

He followed his mother out the door, throwing one last look of warning Levi's way.

Anna watched them leave and the breath rushed out of her. She looked at Levi helplessly, her frustration evident in her voice.

"What am I to do?"

Levi shook his head slightly. "There's not much you can do, Anna. You will not be fit to move from this room for some time."

She stared at him in horror. "I cannot stay here! How is that possible? These people don't know me." One was a Roman, one an outcast Jew. Either one would not hesitate to cause her all kinds of problems if they knew she was a follower of Christ.

Levi settled on the stool that Lucius had vacated. He took Anna's hand, squeezing it with a gentle strength that brought more tears to Anna's eyes. Her mind told her to flee, but her body refused to obey. Levi would surely understand her position better than anyone and give her aid.

He patted her hand, his look suddenly intense.

"Anna, I have a question to ask you and I want you to be honest with me."

She hesitated, her heart pounding with dread. She slowly nodded her head in acquiescence despite the pain it caused.

"Are you a follower of the Way?"

Pinpricks of ice shimmied across her entire body, leaving her cold. Why would he ask such a thing? Her mind couldn't react fast enough to the thoughts flashing through it. How was she to answer? There was really no choice. She had to speak the truth even though her life hung in the balance. Her voice came out little more than a whisper.

"I am."

The sun coming in the open balcony doorway settled on his craggy face, lighting his features as effectively as the joy she saw radiating from him.

"Praise the Lord!" he declared enthusiastically, squeezing her hand more heartily. "I had heard something to that effect when I attended the meetings of the believers, but I never saw you there, so I wasn't certain."

Stunned, Anna could only stare at him in openmouthed amazement. Levi was a believer? She shifted to rise but was reminded of her condition when pain brought her up short. She reluctantly settled back against the cushions.

"I…I couldn't attend. My father…"

Levi nodded sympathetically. "I understand. It was he who beat you so badly?"

It was more a statement than a question, so Anna didn't bother to answer him. He released her hand and rose to his feet.

"I asked you that question because I have something to share with you. The owner of this house is also a believer and she wishes you to find refuge here for as long as you need."

"Your daughter is a follower of the Christ?" The surprises just kept coming. Her mind spun crazily with possibilities.

Anna would love to have been a cricket on the wall in the triclinium to hear the conversation between the two. So that was why they had both looked so full of joy when they entered the room.

Well she could remember when Levi had railed against the Romans and their intermarrying with Jews. His hatred had known no bounds. Now, she understood that anger more fully. He had lost his only child to such a marriage.

And now, he was willing to accept Leah back even though the Jewish community had shunned her. If other people knew, Levi would surely be shunned, as well, except in Bethany where many had become believers because of the man Lazarus. Only the Lord Jesus had the power to overcome such obstinate loathing among her people.

When Levi looked at her again, there was a twinkle in his eye.

"I know you may find this hard to comprehend, but I believe the Lord used you to bring my daughter and me back together again."

The pain that filled her body seemed to lessen at his words. If she had been the instrument used to bring father and daughter together again in the Lord, then everything she had gone through had been worth it.

"A word of warning, though," Levi told her. "Her son is *not* a follower of the Way."

Lucius followed his mother into the peristyle, the sounds of the trickling fountain of the garden doing nothing to soothe his sour mood as it had so many times in the past.

"What is going on, Mother?" he asked without preamble. "How could you send for a man who so ruthlessly cast you from his life?"

His mother seated herself on the stone bench nearest the marble fountain and motioned to the place beside her. Lucius ignored the entreaty, too restless to stay in one position. He began to pace, pushing a hand back through his dark hair in agitation.

A maid who was cleaning the tile walkways quickly gathered her supplies and left at his mother's nod of the head.

Quiet settled in the garden except for the trickling water and the trilling of the songbirds attracted there by the coolness of the temperatures and the availability of water.

"Lucius, there are some things you need to know."

He took a deep breath, knowing he wasn't going to like what she was about to say.

"Go on," he said, turning to her.

She pressed her lips inward against her teeth, taking her time about getting her thoughts in order before hitting him with the one he least expected.

"Lucius, I am a Christian."

His eyes went wide with surprise, his mouth dropping open. Of all the things he had expected her to say, this was certainly not it.

"You can't be serious!"

Leah sighed heavily. "I assure you, I am."

"But...how?" Lucius stopped, not knowing what to say.

How on this piece of downtrodden earth had she come to such a conclusion? He had heard much about this sect of Jews and nothing he had heard had been good. They caused problems wherever they went in the Empire. Fury poured through him, a fury made more dangerous by the fear for his mother.

"I forbid it."

She gave him a look he recognized from childhood, one that said she would humor him, but only up to certain point.

"Please sit down, Son. You make me nervous pacing about like a lion."

He dropped to the seat beside her, his legs suddenly weak. How had she managed to hide such a thing? It hurt him that something so momentous had been kept secret from him. Before he had been sent to Rome, he and his mother had always had a close relationship. They had leaned against each other in order to survive his father's abuse. No one knew what his father had truly been like because he and his mother had, by mutual, unspoken consent, kept such intimate matters confidential. It had forged a bond between them that had lasted throughout the years.

"How long has this been going on?" he asked darkly.

She frowned at him, straightening her red palla around her shoulders. Leaning forward, she pulled a dried bougainvillea leaf from the fountain.

"Nothing is going on!" she chided him. "I became a Christian several years ago. I went to hear the Apostle Peter speak and was convinced that Jesus was the true Son of Elohim."

He leaned his elbows against his knees, pushing the hair back from his forehead with both hands. He released a pent-up breath.

"The Jews would kill you for such a thing." Not to mention the Romans, who hated Christians even more than Jews.

Leah laid a hand against his back and started rubbing slow circles. Instead of calming him, he tensed against her touch.

"Many Jews have come to believe in Him." She paused, her voice lowering. "Even my father."

He jerked his head up, turning to glare at her. "And?"

"We have made our peace," she told him softly.

He jumped up, glaring down at her, fists clenched at his sides. "And just like that, you forgive him?"

Her brown eyes misted with tears as she smiled up at him. "We forgave each other."

"Mother! What did you have to be forgiven for?" He wanted to shake some sense into her. His neat little world was being turned upside down.

She reached out and took his hand, squeezing slightly. He wanted to jerk away but he couldn't bring himself to do so.

"For being a disobedient daughter. For denying my faith. For many things that you can't possibly understand right now."

"You mean because I'm not a Christian."

Her sorrowful brown eyes met his, a sad smile touching her lips. "Yes, because you are not a Christian."

He knelt before her, taking her other hand and unknowingly crushing both hands in his grip.

"Mother, this Jesus was a common criminal who was crucified on a cross. If He was the Son of this God of yours, why would your God allow such a thing?"

"Our Father allowed it for our salvation, Lucius, so that we could spend eternity with Him. Jesus was the sacrificial lamb that took away the sins of the world."

That certainly fit in with his perception of a father. Manipulating. Abusing His power. Could his mother not see that? Could she not see that this God of hers was a tyrant?

He demanded everything from His followers even unto death. He had seen Christians in Rome crucified for refusing to worship Nero as a god. Even here in Jerusalem these Christians had been persecuted and killed. Where was their God then? Terror for his mother clutched at his heart.

"He took away your sins, as well, Lucius. If only you would believe in Him, He has reached out to you in death."

Lucius released her hands and rose to his feet shaking his head. "Don't expect me to worship this God of yours."

"Son, you have been searching for the truth all of your life. You have always had an open mind in your searching. Don't close it now. He wants to be the father that you never had, the kind of father every man should be."

"You want me to be open-minded about this? A father who slays his children?" He shook his head and stepped away from her. "Never. I will never allow such a man to have so much power over me ever again."

He hated the hurt he caused her. "You want me to be open-minded, Mother. But in this I cannot be."

Leah shook her head. "Not just open-minded, Lucius. Openhearted, as well."

He would give his mother the world if he could. He had always been her protector, often taking the beatings on himself that were meant for her. He loved her without measure and would keep her safe in whatever way needed. Even if it meant protecting her from herself.

Chapter 4

Anna sat wrapped in a wool shawl on the balcony above the peristyle enjoying the light, cool breeze that caused her hair to gently tickle the edges of her face. Her skin was kissed by the warmth of the sun and she lifted her face to it, closing her eyes and relishing the contentment that had been missing from her life for a very long time.

The birds trilling in the garden below brought a smile to her face. Although the swelling had receded to a point where she no longer grimaced when she was trying to smile, the yellow-green color of the bruises would take longer to fade.

She leaned over the balustrade and threw to the ground below some of the crumbs she had hoarded from her breakfast. A small ruckus broke out as the sparrows fought for the meager sustenance.

Days had slipped into a week. The pain that she awoke with each day lessened until it was finally bearable for her to move around. All except her ribs, and Levi had told her that would take more time.

She brushed a hand against the saffron-colored tunic that Leah had given her. The generosity of the woman was overwhelming. The silky texture of the robe was almost hypnotic as it glided against her skin, leaving her feeling as though she was wrapped in a silken cocoon. She had never seen such a garment, much less hoped to wear one.

Did it make her look less plain, she wondered? And if so, would a man like Tribune Lucius Tindarium think so? She smiled wryly at such foolish thoughts. She wasn't even sure what had made such an idea pop into her head.

Anna had seen nothing of Lucius for some days, but his charisma seemed to linger in her room, his vitality adding a presence that was missed long after he was gone. Everywhere she looked she could picture his solemn features. She had seen him smile only twice, and even then, his smile did not reach his eyes. She wondered if the man ever smiled unreservedly. She knew without doubt that if he ever did, he would be devastatingly handsome. He was attractive enough without a smile. With one, he would be lethal.

Leah had informed her that Lucius had been called away and would be gone for some time. Anna breathed a sigh of relief at the news. She was uncertain why it was so, but he unsettled her to the point that she could hardly think when she was in his presence. Perhaps it was because he was a Roman but, if she was honest with herself, she would admit that it was not.

It was something altogether different that made her nerves tingle when she was around him. Something that put her senses on guard. Something she wasn't certain if she should fear or not.

Leah, on the other hand, was someone she had quickly grown to love. She was kindness personified. They spent many hours together talking of various things, the most important being the things they had each learned from letters that had been distributed by the various disciples to the house churches in the area. It thrilled them both to have found kindred spirits in each other.

There was a knock on the door and Anna turned to call admittance. Leah entered, her sky-blue tunic flowing gracefully around her, her sandal-shod feet tapping against the marble tiles. She was followed by a maid carrying a tray.

"I thought perhaps you might like some refreshment."

Anna felt a moment's disquiet. Jewish laws of hospitality aside, it didn't sit well with her to be a burden to someone for such a long time. Her father had pounded into her head that she was nothing but a nuisance and now she was proving him right.

"I truly don't wish to be a burden to you," she stated uncomfortably, watching as Leah brought another chair onto the balcony, and then a small table. The maid set the tray on the table and stood back, awaiting instructions.

Leah waved away Anna's objections with a ring-encrusted hand. "Nonsense. Having you here has been one of the greatest blessings Elohim could have bestowed on me."

She turned to the maid, her smile broadening. "Of course, I have Tapat here to keep me company."

Tapat returned her smile. Anna studied the girl closely, noting that she seemed to have an unusual relationship with the mistress of the house that spoke of more than servitude. She didn't act like a slave. Although slavery was permitted among the Jews, it was not widely practiced except among the wealthy. And Leah was obviously wealthy, although it was equally obvious that her wealth had not brought her happiness.

Tapat was not much younger than Anna herself. Her name in Hebrew meant "little girl," and the name fit her well. She was a tiny little thing, even smaller than Anna. The thing that drew Anna to the girl was that she was just as plain in appearance. Anna felt sorry for her and wondered what her story was, but she didn't know her well enough to ask. Although Tapat was the one who had been attending Anna for the last several days, they had spoken very little.

Leah and Anna watched the maid leave the room, and then Leah turned to Anna.

"Tapat is a Christian, as well. That's why I chose her to attend you," Leah told her. "She is more like a daughter to me than a servant."

Relieved, Anna smiled. "I thought she seemed more than just a servant."

Leah nodded, reaching out to pour apricot juice from the jug on the tray into one of the Jerusalem-glass goblets. She handed one to Anna and poured one for herself.

"She was a slave of a man who lost all his possessions. He was about to offer her on the slave market when I happened upon him."

"You bought her?"

Leah nodded again. "And then I gave her her freedom. She stays with me because she has nowhere else to go, and frankly, selfish as it may seem, I am thankful. She has been my one true friend for several years."

Leah had a houseful of servants. Was Tapat then the only Christian? Anna didn't think it her place to pry, but she needed to ask. "Has it been very hard for you living here in Jerusalem?"

When Leah reached forward to hand Anna one of the pastries on the tray, the sunlight cast on her features, letting Anna see the fine lines on her face that, although still beautiful, showed that her age was creeping up on her. If she lived the hard life that Anna could imagine, it would explain the tired lines etched around her mouth. Rich or poor, a life without friends and family was a constant drudgery.

"In some ways," she told Anna, "but in other ways, not so much." She leaned back in her chair and her look became distant.

"When my husband was alive, there were good times, and there were bad. Lucius couldn't understand why I wouldn't leave him." She smiled sadly. "If I had, I would have lost my son and that was something I was not willing to do."

She stared off into the distance for some time, the look on her face showing that her thoughts were far away and not altogether pleasant.

"Your son encouraged you to leave your husband?"

Anna was surprised. Whether Jew or Roman, it was a male-dominated world. Sons rarely sided with a mother against a father.

Leah started slightly, as though she had forgotten Anna's presence for a moment. She glanced at Anna, and then quickly turned away.

"It's not good to speak ill of the dead." She set her goblet on the mosaic-topped table and gave a weak smile. "Let us talk of something more enjoyable than my wretched life and the mistakes I made."

Anna twisted her own goblet in her hands, staring into the golden liquid. She wanted to ask about Levi, but was reluctant to bring up another subject that might be painful to her hostess.

As though she could read Anna's mind, Leah brought the subject up herself. "My father says that your wounds have healed well and that your ribs should be much better in two or three more weeks."

Anna nodded her head. "Yes, it's much easier to breathe even now. I hope I won't have to inconvenience you much longer."

Leah reached across and laid a hand on Anna's. "My dear, you haven't been an inconvenience. I have enjoyed the company more than you can know." The serious look on her face gave credence to the statement.

Although she could barely remember her own mother, Leah was very much like the image Anna had fixed in her mind. It was not so much the looks, more the gentle attitude. The comfortable feeling that you were loved for who you were, and not what was expected of you.

"You are a worshipper of Jesus," Anna stated, wondering if that was so, why Leah was so lonely. "Where then do you meet with other believers?"

The smile Leah gave Anna didn't quite reach her eyes. "I open my house for those who will come."

Anna lifted a brow in inquiry and Leah looked away.

"Jewish prejudices are hard to overcome even among Christians. There are few who will associate with a woman they consider a Roman harlot."

That was certainly true enough. "But you live alone. How can anyone think such a thing now?"

Leah's smile held just a tinge of bitterness. "Some memories are never forgotten."

Anna hadn't known Leah long, but she definitely held no such animosity toward her hostess. How could she when the woman had been nothing but kind?

"How many people come?" Anna finally asked.

Leah twisted the rings on her fingers. "Only Tapat and a few of the other servants."

It was clear to Anna that Leah was a very lonely woman. Christians should not harbor such grudges. The man Leah claimed as her husband was long dead.

"And your father?"

Leah's face lit up, erasing the tired lines. "I told you that I believed you to be an answer to prayer. I have been trying to think of a way to bring my father here so that I could talk to him. Imagine my surprise when I found out that he was a follower of the Way." Her doe-brown eyes glistened with tears. "I have been praying for him, only to find out that he was also praying for me."

Anna smiled. "I had no idea that Levi had become a Christian. He was always so..." Anna hesitated, searching her mind for a word that wouldn't be offensive.

"Pharisaical?" Leah inserted, and they both laughed. That one word said a lot.

"Exactly."

"The Lord works in mysterious ways," Leah said softly.

"Indeed."

They both sat in silence for several seconds. Finally, Leah got to her feet.

"I need to go now. I have things to do, but if you don't mind, I will come back later and have my supper with you."

"I would like that," Anna answered quietly.

She watched the older woman leave the room, the proud tilt of her shoulders belied by the air of loneliness that surrounded her. Anna knew suddenly and instinctively that she had found a friend for life.

Lucius trod the halls of the Antonia Fortress, the building named after the great Marc Antony, until he came to his own apartment. He removed his breastplate, gladius and sword and dumped them on his bed. He glanced about and for the first time in his memory felt discontent. Although his apartment was palatial compared to the other soldiers', it was nothing in comparison to his mother's house.

It wasn't the comfort he missed so much as it was the

atmosphere. The building itself was fully supplied with a gymnasium, heated baths, a meeting hall and various other rooms besides the barracks rooms. Much of the fortress was as elaborate as any wealthy Roman's house. But here there was nothing but cold stone and, even on the brightest day, darkness. And it was a darkness that far transcended absence of light. Here, it was more a darkness of the soul.

He shook his head to rid himself of such thoughts. How had he suddenly become so morbid? He had always been content with his life, if not happy. Why now was he feeling such uneasiness, such restlessness?

Truth be told, it had started after staring into Anna's liquid brown eyes, which seemed to contain all the mysteries of life. Mysteries he longed to delve into, but was afraid to. Mysteries that, it would seem, his mother had already tested.

He sneered at himself. He couldn't remember a time when he was afraid, not even in the midst of battle, but now…

What was he so afraid of? A dead carpenter? One thing he had learned long ago was that to overcome a fear, you had to first face it. With that thought in mind, he decided to pay his mother a visit after he removed some of the Judean grime from his body.

He had been gone three weeks now and he had missed his mother more than usual. But, then again, it wasn't his mother's face that continually haunted his dreams. It surprised him that he was so anxious to see how Anna had fared in his absence.

He headed for the baths, deciding to bypass the tepidarium's lukewarm water and chose instead the hot water of the caldarium. His body needed the intense heat to relax his tired muscles.

He passed the palaestra where several soldiers were

practicing battle moves. Their well-toned bodies gleamed with sweat from their hours of exercise. They paused and quickly saluted him, and he returned their salute. As a tribune in Rome's army, he felt a fierce pride in his men.

Several of the men who had returned with him from this last assignment were already in the caldarium. Their chatter echoed in the large tiled room. They greeted him respectfully, and he returned their greetings with a wave.

He found a less-occupied spot and removed his sandals and the blood-red tunic that proclaimed his occupation, placing them in the cubbyholes provided.

He stepped into the pool and allowed the hot water to roll over his aching body. He leaned back against the mosaic tiles, his body relaxing but his mind refusing to do likewise.

It had been a grueling three weeks. Under the guise of building Roman roads, he had been given the assignment of searching out a band of zealots that was beginning to cause a problem here in Judea. Roman tolerance of the Jews was quickly fading with the assassinations of several leading Romans who had lived here in Jerusalem. Tempers were beginning to flare on both sides.

Discontent among the Jewish population was feeding a fast-growing rebellion against the empire. Finding the zealots, though, was proving more difficult than he had anticipated. Normally, a few gold coins gracing someone's palm would lead to the information he needed, but lately, the Jews had joined forces against what they considered a common enemy.

Andronicus joined him in the water, leaning back nonchalantly against the side of the bath. Although Andronicus's muscled body seemed relaxed, there was a tenseness about him that communicated itself to Lucius. Lucius lifted a brow, but said nothing. If Andronicus was searching him out, something was on his mind.

Scanning the area, Andronicus could see that no one was paying attention to them. The look he gave Lucius set Lucius's heart to thrumming with anticipation. He was familiar with that look, and it boded ill for the person receiving it.

"There's something I think you should know," Andronicus told him grimly. "I have spoken with my informants in the city, and I believe your mother might be in danger."

Lucius's body went cold all over, then just as quickly fired with heat. If anything happened to his mother he would tear this city apart to find the miscreant who did it.

"What are you saying?" Lucius asked, his voice equally grim.

Andronicus shifted slightly under his regard, uncomfortable brown eyes meeting cold steel-gray ones.

"The zealots believe her to be a Roman sympathizer. That fire at her house last week was no accident."

Lucius growled deep in his throat and rose from the water, all thoughts of relaxation forgotten. He felt his body tense for battle and realized this was a battle he couldn't hope to win when he was so often gone from Jerusalem. He had to get his mother out of here. Another battle he would have to fight, for she had always refused to leave her homeland.

He glanced down at Andronicus. "Thank you, my friend."

Andronicus gave him a hard look. "If you need any help, just let me know."

Lucius nodded. Placing his palms against the walkway surrounding the pool, he lifted himself out of the water.

A servant handed him a strigil, but he chose instead the towel the man held in his other hand. He had no time for the instrument used to scrape away the water. Something in his gut told him time was of the essence.

Chapter 5

Anna and Leah wandered through the crowded market-place streets, the lanes made even smaller by the horde of people filling Jerusalem in preparation for Passover.

The cacophonous sounds of vendors selling their wares mingled with people haggling over prices, along with a multitude of squawking chickens, bleating goats and sheep and a host of other livestock.

The shrill cry of kites added to the din as they circled above the city in the vivid blue sky. Small puffs of white clouds ambled slowly across the blue expanse, giving a lazy feel to the warm spring day.

It was the first time Anna had been away from Leah's house and she was enjoying the freedom. Not that she didn't appreciate her hostess's hospitality, but it felt good to be outside the villa listening to the life all around her.

Many members of the trade guilds wandered through the crowds, their occupations easily spotted by the emblems of their trade. Anna recognized a tailor by the bone needle stuck in his cloak. He was arguing with a dyer of cloth, also easily recognized by the brightly colored tag of cloth attached to his cloak.

Leah was headed for the baker's district. There was a baker there who was of the Way and Leah liked to give the man her business. She could have easily sent one of the servants, but Leah liked to wander the markets herself. Anna wondered if it made her less lonely to be among such a throng.

Anna's ribs were still slightly tender, but the rest of her had healed well. Levi had returned several times and had pronounced her healthy enough to be up and about. The only problem she was having was when she was jostled by the crowd, but she wouldn't for the world have mentioned it to Leah. Such a day was worth a little pain.

It had been good to witness the growing bond between Levi and his daughter as a result of his caring for Anna during her recovery. Anna's own heart had always longed for just such a relationship, but it had been denied her. That was, until she had found the Lord. She heartily embraced the loving Father she had learned about from the disciples of Jesus.

Leah's happiness over the increasing relationship with her father was communicated in the way she perpetually smiled. Anna was so happy for her. Even now Leah walked along, her lips tilted up in joy, the blue-colored tunic and yellow palla making her look like a ray of sunshine.

As for herself, while she knew she could never be considered lovely, the light blue tunic she wore gave her a feeling of confidence that the rags she had worn before had stripped her of. The new leather sandals on her feet tapped along the packed-dirt street, making her feel as though she were walking on air.

They continued to meander through the marketplace, Leah finding items she just couldn't do without. The basket on Leah's arm continued to fill until Anna was afraid it would soon become too heavy for the older woman to bear. Anna believed it was more a way of helping the poor who struggled each day for their very survival than any real desire for the products Leah purchased.

Conversation stopped whenever they approached a booth. Suspicious looks were constantly thrown their way. From the way Leah dressed, one would assume she was a Roman, and it was rare for a wealthy Roman to be in this part of the city. Anna began to feel a little uneasy at the continued baleful stares.

Her unease must have communicated itself to Leah. The older woman glanced her way, the lines on her face more pronounced as she frowned.

"Is something wrong, Anna?"

Anna tried to reassure her with a smile. If Leah noticed nothing untoward, then Anna didn't want to alarm her.

"No, nothing."

"Are you tired, my dear? I'm so sorry. I should have realized."

Anna laid a hand on Leah's arm. She didn't want to be the cause of ruining this lovely outing.

"Truly, Leah. I am fine."

Leah started to say something when she was interrupted by a loud voice that reverberated above the commotion around them.

"So, there you are."

The warm, sunny day chilled dramatically as Anna's body went cold all over at a voice she all too easily recognized. She froze in place, her eyes widening in alarm as she tried to get her numb brain to get the message to her feet to flee. And then, it was too late. She turned in time to see her father bearing down upon her. His face was a black thundercloud, his eyes shooting daggers. Her body tingled with fear, her blood running through her veins like a river of ice.

Looking from one to the other, Leah recognized the danger and stepped boldly into her father's path, causing him to come to an abrupt halt.

His menacing glare moved from Anna to Leah, his bushy eyebrows lifting upward. "Get out of my way, woman!"

Anna tried to move Leah to the side, but the woman wouldn't be budged. If Leah was hurt because of her, Anna would never be able to forgive herself.

"Leah, please."

The crowd around them increased as people turned to stare, and it was obvious their sympathy was not with the richly dressed woman. Murmurs grew louder, faces angrier, but Leah ignored them, focusing instead on the fuming man before her. She drew herself up to her full height, which was only slightly larger than Anna's petite frame.

"Who are you, and how dare you order me about!"

Beetling brows drew down in fury. "My name is Abiyram Benyamin and I am this woman's father." He glowered at Anna. "I have been searching everywhere for you. You're coming home with me."

He started to reach past Leah, but Leah slapped his hand away.

"She will do no such thing! She is staying with me."

Startled at Leah's audacity, Anna's father stood silent, but only for a moment. With a growl, he shoved Leah to the side, causing her to fall to the ground, and grabbed Anna by her wrist. He jerked her forward and Anna sucked in a breath at the sharp pain that tore through her side. She struggled against her father's painful grip, flinching when he raised his hand to strike her.

"Hold!"

The one word rang with authority around the small, crowded square. Silence descended on the people, the only noise now coming from the animals in the area. The sudden quiet that settled over the square after the previous cacophony was eerie.

Anna saw Lucius striding through the crowd, his face distorted by anger. He exuded such an aura of violence, people hastily stepped out of his way. All eyes were on him as he approached, an impressive man despite being without his army accoutrement.

When he reached his mother, he bent quickly to help her to her feet. His glacial eyes searched for any injury.

"Are you all right?"

The softness of his voice was belied by the angry tic working in his jaw.

She nodded, brushing down her tunic with trembling hands. Lucius set her to the side, turning to where Abiyram still held Anna captive.

Lucius's composed features were even more intimidating than his earlier anger. His eyes glittered with rage, his nostrils flaring, but he impressively managed to hold himself in check. Anna considered his frozen features, taking note of the feral gleam in his eyes, and thought that that must be what it was like to look death in the face. Her father must have finally realized the same thing. He quickly stepped back, some of the bluster leaving him.

"What has this to do with you, Roman?"

The belligerence in Abiyram's voice brought heated color to Lucius's face. Lucius stepped so close that his face was a mere hairbreadth away from Abiyram's.

"This woman is my mother," he growled softly, "and you will beg her forgiveness before I have the skin stripped from your back and have you thrown into prison."

The very quietness of Lucius's voice sent a shiver down Anna's back. She glanced at her father to see his reaction. Did he know just what jeopardy he was in? She barely knew Lucius, yet she knew without doubt that her father was in imminent danger. That was no idle threat. Even the crowd around them began to back away as they realized that they could be considered accomplices to her father's act.

Anna swallowed hard at the intense hatred emanating from her father's eyes. It seemed as though hours passed as the two men continued to stare at each other. Anna knew that her father would never beg anything from a woman, much less a Roman. But, surprisingly, just when she thought the tension had reached a breaking point, he relented. Or as close as he would ever come to doing so.

He glanced at Leah balefully. "My pardon," he told her icily.

Leah seemed to notice for the first time the stares of the crowd around her. She shifted uneasily as she recognized the threat to her son. She nodded at Anna's father.

Abiyram reached again for Anna but Lucius stepped between them. Abiyram's brows furrowed with his returning anger.

"This woman is my daughter. She has run away from home and I have come to take her back."

Lucius continued to stare coldly at Abiyram until the older man once again retreated a step. Leah stepped around him, placing a protective arm around Anna's shoulder and hugging her tightly.

Anna was comforted by the reassurance, but she didn't wish to be the cause of anything happening to Leah or her son. The murmurs of the crowd were growing again. If the mob were to attack, Anna had no doubt that they would all be killed. They were alone here among the hostile gathering.

"I found this woman in the desert severely beaten and took her to my mother's for care," Lucius told Abiyram through gritted teeth, his glance raking the crowd around them. His control seemed tenuous at best. "If I hadn't found her, she would have died."

Abiyram looked from Lucius to Anna. His lips curled into a sneer. "It would seem she has been well taken care of."

Anna's face colored hotly at the implication. She saw Lucius's hands fist at his sides, but his voice when he spoke was almost friendly.

"Indeed."

He said no more, merely standing in Abiyram's way, his arms folded across his chest. Abiyram shifted uneasily as the standoff continued.

"I will relieve you of your obligation now," Abiyram told him snidely, but made no move toward Anna. When Lucius didn't move or speak, Abiyram reached for Anna again.

Anna felt her heart drop to her toes. After all she had been through, was it truly Elohim's will for her to go back to such a life of brutality? The scriptures said for children to obey their parents, and she had fought with herself many times over the desire to stay in His will. Was she truly dishonoring Elohim by defying Abiyram?

Leah made a move to speak, but Lucius silenced her with a slight movement of his hand.

"Not so fast," Lucius told Abiyram, causing him to hesitate once again. Abiyram turned to Lucius ready to argue further, but Lucius forestalled him.

"There is the matter of repayment."

Abiyram's eyes went wide. "I never asked you to care for her," he spat out.

"Nonetheless, it was done."

Lucius's calm only seemed to enrage her father further.

"I won't pay you a single denarius," Abiyram snarled, pushing back his cloak and placing his fists against his hips. His portly belly pushed against his tunic.

Lucius looked down, seemingly intent on picking a thread from the bottom of his blood-red tunic. When he looked up again, his eyes were black with rage.

"Shall we take the matter before procurator Felix?"

Lucius's voice was still quiet, but Anna could tell he was only a heartbeat away from violence. She would truly hate to have that anger directed toward her. The man must be like an avenging angel on the battlefield.

Her father, though, also seemed on the verge of violence. His face was almost purple with equal amounts of rage. Yet he knew that to go before the procurator was tantamount to going before Rome, and Rome was not likely to side against her own. In fact, it was more likely that her father would be arrested as an insurrectionist with hostilities between the two countries at an all-time high.

Abiyram's lips pressed tightly together. "How much?"

The smile Lucius gave Abiyram made him swallow hard.

"Thirty pieces of silver should cover it."

Abiyram's face turned white and Anna's eyes went wide. Thirty pieces of silver was the usual price for a slave. Is that what Lucius was suggesting? Had this been his intention all along?

Abiyram's mouth opened and closed several times before he was able to push words from his mouth.

"I don't have that kind of money."

"Then perhaps I could take *you* in payment until your debt is paid."

Abiyram quailed at the look on Lucius's face despite his own escalating anger.

Anna watched her father's struggle. She knew as well

as her father that Lucius was only hoping for something
to happen. Every muscle in the Roman's body was tense,
ready to avenge his mother's mistreatment.

Her father's hands clenched into fists. He glared at Lucius for several long seconds before he finally spat out,
"Keep her then." He glared at Anna. "Prostitute yourself
on the streets for all I care, but don't ever think you can
come crawling back to me when these Romans tire of you."

Turning, he pushed his way through the crowd and disappeared from their view.

Lucius watched Anna's father walk away through a red
haze of fury. He glared after the man, his hand clutching
the gladius at his side. Even when he had gone into battle with his blood running like a river of hot lava, he had
not hungered to kill a man as he did right at this minute.
It would be so easy to pull his gladius from its sheath and
throw it into the man's retreating back. Being an expert in
the art, he knew he would not miss and Anna would be
free from the man forever.

He was angrier than he could ever remember being in
his life, even those times that he had suffered at the hands
of his own father. His fierce warrior's blood was on the boil
and if he didn't soon find a target for his pent-up rage he
was liable to do something he would later regret.

His mother laid a restraining hand on his arm and he
felt the heat in his blood cool ever so slowly until he could
focus on her standing at his side, a worried expression on
her face.

"Let it go, Lucius."

He realized that she was talking about more than just
this encounter. Every time he thought he had finally conquered his own personal nightmares, something would
transpire to show him otherwise.

He chanced a look at Anna and couldn't begin to fathom the expressions crossing her face, the two uppermost being fear and, conversely, appreciation. Was the fear of him, or what might have happened had he not intervened?

Taking Leah and Anna each by an arm in a gentle yet inexorable grip, he started moving them through the increasing crowd of gawkers and turned them toward the upper city. People hastily moved out of his way as he plunged through the multitude.

When he reached his mother's villa, he pushed them through the door, slamming it behind him. He was breathing hard, but not from exertion. Seeing the fading bruises on Anna's arms had set his mind to thinking on things best left alone, but as always, his struggle was more against himself. The anger that had faded at his mother's touch was returning with a vengeance.

"Stay put," he commanded them both.

His mother's eyes went wide at his tone of voice, but since he'd never spoken to her in such a way before, she wisely remained silent.

He reached for the door handle, but his mother's voice halted him.

"Where are you going?"

He didn't turn. Clenching the handle tighter, he tried to get a grip on his emotions. Closing his eyes, he took a deep breath.

"I'm going to the barracks. If I don't see you again today, please don't leave the house."

He gave her a look then that she well understood. She nodded and he left.

Chapter 6

It was several days before Lucius was able to make it back to his mother's house. When he arrived, the door was bolted from the inside, causing alarm to pierce through him. His mother had never bolted the door before, preferring to use the iron lock that Lucius had a spare key for.

Pounding on the portal, he quickly glanced around, looking for signs of trouble. Seeing nothing out of the ordinary, he relaxed only slightly.

The small door fixed inside the larger portal slid back and a servant peered out. Something else newly instituted, making him tense again. He heard the servant quickly slide back the bolt on the inside and open the door.

He pushed past her into the house, quickly scanning the atrium. He glanced down at the girl and realized that although she had recognized him, he had not done likewise. She must be a fairly new servant. He sighed inwardly. His mother was forever adding to her household people in various kinds of trouble. Her generosity frightened him, especially with all the unrest in Jerusalem right now. He would have to talk to her about it. She had no idea the danger she might be bringing into her home. Things here in this city were on the boil and it was only a matter of time before the pot spewed over.

"My mother? She is well?" His voice came out harsher than he intended and the girl's eyes widened in alarm.

"Yes, m'lord. She is in the peristyle."

Releasing a slow breath, Lucius felt his worry lessen. He quietly moved through the atrium into the peristyle beyond.

He was brought up short by the sight of his mother and Anna sitting on the marble bench beside the fountain, heads close together, in deep, animated discussion. They didn't hear him enter, so engrossed were they, so he took a moment to study them.

His mother looked better than he had seen her for some time. The joy that had been missing from her life seemed to have found its way back in again. Was that because of Anna, or had something else transpired that he had no knowledge of? He was guiltily reminded of how lonely she had been, how much she had depended on his society. He had tried to attend her as much as possible, but he was here in Jerusalem because he had a job to do.

His eyes slid to Anna and he felt a little jolt at the sight of her. So angry had he been at the marketplace, he had failed to notice her altered appearance. He couldn't decide just what it was that had changed though, because her looks hadn't changed that much outwardly in just a few days. He frowned, leaning against the doorframe. What then was there about her that brought on a sudden quickening of his pulse?

She would never be considered lovely, but the gentleness she exuded was captivating in an elemental kind of way. Just being in her presence was like being covered with a balm of myrrh and just as exhilarating. How could someone remain so gentle of spirit having come from such a harsh situation? He had instead grown bitter and angry. The woman intrigued him, and that's something that hadn't happened in a long while.

When he shifted position, his gladius tapped against the frame and alerted them to his presence. They both turned, his mother getting quickly to her feet. Her face lit with pleasure.

"Lucius! Come in!"

Anna schooled her expression so quickly he hadn't a hope of interpreting it.

He bent to receive his mother's kiss on his cheek. He searched carefully for any outward sign of distress.

"You are well?"

She smiled, but her face registered her confusion. "Of course. Why do you ask?"

His eyes narrowed with suspicion. "Why then have you started bolting the door?"

Her face cleared. "Oh, that. I was afraid Anna's father might try to come for her."

Lucius's lips twitched as he tried to hide his smile. His mother could be a bear when she was protecting her family, and for some reason, she had included Anna in that category.

"I don't think you will have to worry on that account, but if anything should happen, I want you to send word to me immediately."

She squeezed his arm reassuringly. "I will. Now, can you stay for supper?"

He hadn't planned to, but one look at Anna and he quickly changed his mind. His eyes met his mother's and he knew that she had caught him staring at the woman with more interest than usual. She glanced from him to Anna and back again and a slow smile graced her face. In that moment something happened that hadn't happened in many years: his face colored with embarrassment.

The smile on his mother's face grew and a twinkle entered her normally somber brown eyes. Lucius sighed inwardly. He was never going to hear the end of this.

Anna rose to her feet, and the soft wool tunic she wore molded against her body as she gracefully moved toward them. Proper nourishment had begun to change her gangly form into one of a nubile young woman. Lucius's breathing suddenly became restricted and he had to quickly look away.

"I'll tell Magog that Lucius will be staying," she told them.

As she passed him, Lucius stopped her by gently grasping her forearm. The scent of myrrh that had been in his thoughts earlier wafted up to him. He was right. It was intoxicating. But he was also wrong. There was certainly no soothing balm that filled his mind. The scent along with the warmth of her skin against his rough palms made his pulse jump erratically.

Her gaze meshed with his and the darkening of her pupils alerted him to the fact that she was just as disturbed as he. Her confusion mirrored his own. Many women far lovelier than Anna had tried unsuccessfully to catch his interest, yet without even trying, she had not only caught it, but firmly held on to it. He was still trying to figure out why this was so. Clearing his throat, he finally managed to speak.

"And after you tell him that, tell him that I wish to see him in the bibliotheca right away."

Anna's brown eyes widened and he realized that although the words were innocuous enough, his tone must have relayed itself. The steward had some explaining to do.

"I will," Anna agreed, and he reluctantly released her. He watched her walk away, her hips swaying gently with the grace of a gazelle.

"Ahem."

Caught again. He gave his mother a look that sent her into peals of laughter.

"Don't say it," he ordered.

She widened her eyes innocently and he shook his head, rolling his eyes upward.

Her look suddenly turned sober, her voice taking on an authority he seldom heard from her. "You mustn't blame Magog for what happened at the market."

The anger he thought he had managed to quench struggled to rise again. It had taken two hours of sparring with the best of his legionnaires to work his rage out of his system. Even then, he knew it was merely buried below the surface, awaiting a convenient time to come forth.

"He's lucky I don't have him whipped, Mother." His voice lacked the heat he had expected.

She regarded him in a fashion that let him know he would never win this argument. The two of them had been playing a game of checks and balances for years. He was determined to protect her, she to protect him, even if it meant protecting him from himself.

He kissed her cheek and smiled. "Don't worry. I only plan to speak with him."

Anna returned to the peristyle, passing him in the doorway. He didn't miss the fact that she stepped far to the side to avoid coming into close proximity with him. A predatory smile crossed his lips. *You can run, little one, but you will never be able to hide from me.* The look she gave him assured him that she had received his nonverbal message. In a word, she was terrified, which did nothing at all for his ego.

He saw Magog crossing the atrium toward the bibliotheca and he moved to join him. The giant Philistine looked uneasy, as well he might. Lucius was not in a very forthcoming mood.

Most of the rooms that adjoined the atrium had open doorways; the bibliotheca did not. He had specifically chosen it because he hadn't wanted anyone else to hear what he had to say to the steward. He closed the door with a decisive click.

Magog preempted what he was about to say.

"I'm sorry, Master. I should have been with my lady in the marketplace."

Lucius crossed the room and seated himself behind the desk he used to conduct business. He leaned back in a chair, folding his arms across his chest.

"And why weren't you?"

The other man sighed, his embarrassment adding to his ruddy complexion. Lucius knew it bothered the man that he had failed in his duty.

"As steward, she asked me to stay behind and oversee the mosaicians as they retiled the triclinium."

Lucius blinked. What was his mother up to now? To retile the triclinium would mean weeks of disorder, and just when he had decided to sell this villa. Magog could probably tell him what else was going on, but that would have to come later. Right now, he needed to make his position perfectly clear. He picked up the stylus he used for writing transactions and twirled it in his fingers.

"I hired you as a bodyguard," he reminded. "Being a steward is secondary."

"I understand, m'lord, but your mother doesn't."

Pressing his lips tightly together, Lucius shook his head.

How was he to answer that one? It was true enough. His mother had always been a law unto herself.

"Regardless," he stated firmly, "you will not allow my mother to leave this house without your attendance ever again. Do I make myself clear?"

Magog lifted an eyebrow. "And you will make this clear to your mother?"

The audacity of the man! Lucius noted the twinkle in the other man's eyes and pushed down his rising irritation. Magog had been with them for several years and his loyalty had never been called into question. In fact, just the reverse. When it came to his mother, the man was usually like a lion protecting its cub. He wondered just what subterfuge his mother had used to get around him. If Lucius was no match for her games, the Philistine certainly wasn't.

"I will make it clear to her, have no fear."

The smile the Philistine was trying to hide told Lucius more than anything what he thought of his success on such an arrangement. ·

"You may go, Magog. But remember what I said." He hesitated to mention his fears, but then he thought it would be wiser to give the man some idea of what he might be up against.

"Sources close to me have alerted me to the fact that my mother may be in danger from sicarii assassins."

Magog's stance went rigid, his eyes taking on a feral gleam. His hand curved around his scimitar, the curved sword glinting ominously. His eyes met Lucius's with deadly purpose.

"Thank you for alerting me, m'lord."

Lucius leaned forward. "And another thing. If a man named Abiyram Benyamin comes anywhere near my mother or Anna…"

He left the sentence hanging, but the Philistine nodded his head in understanding, his dark eyes glinting.

Lucius watched him leave and felt some of the terror leave that had encased his heart ever since Andronicus's announcement. Forewarned was forearmed, and Magog would be a lethal enemy.

Anna watched Lucius go into the triclinium, her heart thrumming violently when she remembered their earlier encounter. She hadn't missed the predatory look in his eyes and was amazed that he would even consider her worthy of notice.

What was there about her that would instill such a reaction? She had heard many tales of Romans and their lustful ways. They even practiced prostitution in their temples to their gods. Even here in Jerusalem there were prostitutes displaying their wares on the streets whom Roman soldiers took full advantage of. But why would he look at *her* that way?

When Lucius had taken her by the arm earlier she had grown warm with a feeling she didn't understand. Her experience with men was minimal, and she had no idea how to react to the present situation. Perhaps it would be better for her to leave, but then where would she go?

Still, she couldn't continue to stay here forever. There were limits to hospitality.

Lucius left the triclinium and entered the peristyle. Their looks collided and her insides started doing that little dance that immediately put her on guard. She knew without doubt that it would take very little for him to storm the ramparts of her defenses. It was time to fortify her barricades, and she had a feeling that it would take more than just prayer.

He noticed a table with chairs near the fountain. One

eyebrow lifted in inquiry. "Where is my mother? Are we to eat out here?"

Anna clasped her hands behind her back. "Your mother will join us momentarily, and yes, we eat out here since your mother is having the floor in the triclinium retiled."

He moved closer and it took everything within her power to keep from stepping away. One thing she did know about predators: running away only made you more of a target.

He stopped in front of her and a slow smile tilted his lips. Was that approval she saw in his eyes?

"So, Anna," he began, his throaty voice sending chills up her spine. "How are you doing?"

To break contact with his compelling eyes, she moved to the bench near the fountain and sat down. She ran her fingers lightly through the cool water, allowing her time to think of something safe to say.

"I am doing much better, as you can see."

"And your ribs?"

He came and sat next to her, sending all her good intentions flying out of the garden. There was no way she could look him in the eyes and keep her composure, so she continued to watch her fingers trailing through the water, smiling when a fish came and began nibbling them.

"My ribs are almost healed. They pain me some if I move too abruptly, but nothing I can't handle."

"I can well imagine," he agreed, his voice taking on a more somber timbre. "It's amazing to me that you managed to travel in the desert, in the dead of night, in such a condition as I found you. You are truly a remarkable woman."

Surprised, she finally looked at him and could see that he was sincere. It pleased her that he regarded her that way. At the same time, she wondered exactly what was so notable about running away. She doubted this man ran from anything.

Leah came into the peristyle and the tense atmosphere immediately lightened. Lucius rose to greet her and she went to him and kissed him on the cheek.

"So, did you get everything settled with Magog?"

Lucius stared down at his mother with a look that was a mixture of love, aggravation and, very nearly, desperation.

"Mother, if you have any feelings for Magog at all, you won't ever again force him to choose between my will and yours."

Leah wrinkled her nose at him, but refused to comment. Lucius allowed the moment to pass. He chose instead another subject.

"Why are you having the triclinium retiled? The workmanship that was there was beautiful."

Leah motioned for them to all take chairs around the table. Since they were eating in the garden and not the triclinium, chairs worked much better than reclining couches.

"The workmanship was beautiful, yes, but I didn't like the design."

Lucius was astounded. She had lived in this house since before he was born, and she just now decided she didn't like the design? He tried to remember what picture was represented, but it had been so long since he had paid any real attention to it that it just wouldn't clearly come to mind. If he remembered correctly, it was something to do with men and women dining at tables, an appropriate design for the triclinium. He had thought the artist's use of tiles representing leftover pieces of food scattered throughout the design particularly appropriate, as it helped to hide the effects of the real food that diners threw on the floor.

Since his father had died, there had been plenty of opportunity for her to change things to her liking; why now? He knew her Jewish sensibilities had been offended by what she considered graven images, but bowing to her heritage, his father had at least made certain the figures were clothed, which was more than could be said of many Roman homes.

Lucius could understand her desire to change things, but why all of a sudden? His intuition told him there was something going on that he needed to check into further, but that would have to wait. He was scheduled to leave again in two days' time and he wasn't certain how long he would be gone.

He studied his mother again, her animated chatter with Anna bringing a smile to his face. The light from the descending sun was muted even more by the shade of the acacia trees surrounding the peristyle, fading the lines on her face until she looked like the mother he remembered from his childhood. Soft and beautiful. Perhaps it was his mother's and Anna's God after all that had brought Anna into their lives. The arrangement seemed to be working out to both of their benefits.

At the marketplace, he had suggested thirty pieces of silver to Abiyram to pay for Anna's care, not fully realizing the price he was asking. The price of a slave. Did he really see Anna that way? And if it came down to it, would he have the courage to claim her as one if it would fit the needs of his mother?

Anna looked his way and his heart began beating faster. The fact that he could claim her by rights left him suddenly without breath.

His gaze returned to his mother and his racing thoughts suddenly stilled. He knew without a doubt that his mother would be horrified at such a suggestion. She didn't approve of slavery and had set all of her servants free after his father died. No, he could never hurt his mother that way, nor, for that matter, Anna. But he would do whatever was necessary, by whatever means necessary, to make certain that Anna stayed, and he knew that it wasn't just because of his mother.

"Well, Mother, I don't want you making any other changes to the villa," he told her, his tone brooking no argument. "I have decided to sell it."

Both women stared at him in astonishment, but it was his mother who spoke.

"What do you mean, you intend to sell it? Where do you plan for me to live?"

He took a deep breath, readying himself for the battle to come.

"I've been recalled to Rome, and I'm taking you with me."

Chapter 7

Anna helped to set the platters of food on the long table in the newly restored triclinium in preparation for the Lord's Day worship. The tile floor now had a flourishing design of leaves and pomegranates, much better than the previous design to Anna's way of thinking. Absurd as it was, she had always felt as if she were trampling on people's faces when she walked across the floor.

Leah had wanted to change the murals on the walls, as well, but after Lucius's declaration about selling the villa she had hesitated to do so.

They had taken their argument to the bibliotheca, but despite a solid door, their heated exchange had penetrated out into the atrium. Anna had moved farther into the peristyle to avoid eavesdropping, so she had no idea what had been decided.

Tapat handed her the goatskin of wine for the observance of the Lord's Supper that Jesus had instituted the night before he died. It was Anna's favorite part of worship.

Anna laid the wineskin on the table, smiling at the fact that it was obviously new. Magog had purchased wine the week before that had been placed in an old wineskin, and the skin had ruptured due to the new wine's fermentation. The resulting mess all over the floor of the kitchen had left the steward severely out of sorts realizing that he had been duped.

Tapat was lighting the braziers located around the room to dispel some of the gloom and add some warmth to the chill brought on by the rain that was even now pounding on the tiled roof. The dry season would soon be upon them, but for now, the water was enjoyed by all as it refreshed the land.

Except, why did it have to be today of all days? Anna sighed. Leah had so been looking forward to this day. Her father intended to join her in worshipping the Lord for the first time since they had been reunited. It was the main reason that she had wanted to retile the floor, so that he wouldn't be offended by the graven images in the design.

Now, it looked as though all Leah's preparations had been for naught. Surely Levi, at his age, wouldn't travel all the way from Bethany to Jerusalem in such weather.

Water was cascading from the opening in the atrium roof to the small pool below provided for that purpose. If the rain continued at this rate, the pool would overflow very soon.

Leah came into the peristyle after warning some of the servants to keep an eye on the atrium's pool and prepare to remove the water if it rose too high. She glanced around, making certain everything was to her satisfaction.

She smiled halfheartedly at Anna, and Anna could see that her enthusiasm for today's proceedings had ebbed due to the weather. Leah had grown accustomed to worshipping with only her servants, yet she had induced her father to come and worship with her instead of with the band of believers in Bethany. Her disappointment must be intense.

Anna gave her a reassuring smile in return. "Regardless of the weather, this is the Lord's Day, a time to worship and praise Him."

Leah sighed. "I know, but I so wanted my father to come." She glanced around the peristyle, sighing again. Even the muted lighting brought on by the rainy weather couldn't dim the beauty of the dining room or hide the preparations that had been made for this special day.

Anna wanted to ask what decision had been made about the villa, but she was afraid to. If Lucius was selling this house and taking his mother to Rome, Anna needed to make plans for what to do, as well. Although it had been on her mind for some time, she had allowed herself to float along on a tranquil sea of contentment, reluctant to make any plans for a future she just couldn't see.

For the first time since waking up in this villa after her escape from her father, she realized just how alone she was. None of her relatives would welcome her after defying her father. Besides, none of them could afford an extra mouth to feed. Without a husband, she had no way to support herself besides selling herself on the street, and she would rather starve to death than resort to that life.

She had even been toying with the idea of selling herself into slavery, but that would be a last resort. There was always the option of sitting at the city gates and begging like so many others did every day, but that didn't agree well with her either.

Forcing down the feelings of self-pity, she thought instead about what this would mean for Leah, as well.

Rome. Throne place of Satan. Was there anywhere on

earth that could be worse for a Christian? Here in Jerusalem the persecution had been terrible enough, but the Romans believed that Jews were atheists because they refused to worship the multitude of gods that had been incorporated into the empire. Persecution there was rising from all the accounts she had heard, and she doubted that it was going to lessen any time soon.

A pounding on the door interrupted her thoughts. She and Leah exchanged surprised looks. The hope that blossomed on Leah's face faded just as quickly as it appeared. The same thought must have occurred to her. Surely Levi wouldn't travel over six miles in this weather.

Tapat went to answer the door, sliding back the inner door and peering out. Recognizing the person on the other side, she quickly slid back the bolt and threw open the portal.

Magog was close beside her, his hand fondling his scimitar, but when Leah's father entered, the surprised steward motioned for a servant to hurriedly bring a basin of water to wash Levi's muddy feet.

Leah was already hastening across the atrium. "Father, I didn't think you were coming." Her tone went from excited to disapproving. "You shouldn't have come. You will surely be made ill by the chill wetness."

Levi waved a hand disparagingly. "I'm a lot stronger than I look. I will be fine."

Leah turned to one of the servants. "Bring some extra towels and a dry tunic. Quickly."

Levi turned to a man standing behind him and motioned him inside. "I have brought a friend, if that is all right with you."

The odiferous aroma of the man preceded him. There was only one occupation Anna knew of that would cause such a scent to be imbedded in even the clothing that he wore.

The tanner was hesitant to enter, and no wonder. Tanners were considered the lowest of the low, refused entrance even to the synagogue because of their occupation dealing with dead animals. The chemicals they used for preparing skins had some of the strongest, most ill-smelling scents imaginable, which didn't endear them to the community either. In fact, the wife of a tanner was permitted to divorce him for such reasons.

The man stood humbly by the door, fully expecting to be rejected. Anna's heart immediately went out to him.

Leah hesitated but a moment, wrinkling her nose when a rain-drenched breeze blew the man's scent across the room. Swallowing hard, she took the man by the arm and pulled him into the room.

"Please, come in." She took a towel from Tapat and handed it to the tanner. She gave him a smile. "May we know your name?"

They could see him more fully now, though much of his face was hidden by the head shawl he wore. He was not old, but neither was he young. What little they could see of his bearded face colored hotly when his eyes connected with Leah's.

"My name is Adoniram."

Leah turned to Tapat. "Bring another dry tunic."

The expression on Tapat's face was amusing. It was apparent that she was holding her breath but trying not to make it obvious. Nodding her head, she hurried away to do as told.

Leah turned to Adoniram, struggling to keep her face from contorting at the offensive smells emanating from the man. The rain had only intensified the odor.

"My steward will show you and my father where you

can change out of those wet garments. If you wish, you can make use of the caldarium to warm yourself before you dress."

The way Leah had suggested using the hot bath would relieve any offense if the man chose to take advantage of it.

Adoniram obviously didn't know what to think at this act of civility. He nodded his head, dropping his eyes and following the steward from the room. Leah's father gave her an approving smile before following after them.

When they were out of sight Leah turned to one of the other servants.

"Michael, add some incense to the braziers. Not too much, mind you."

She turned to Anna. "Are you all right having the tanner in our midst?"

Surprised, Anna told her sharply, "Of course."

Leah smiled. "I thought you would be." She stared at the door the tanner had disappeared through, her thoughts reflecting on her face. Her empathy with Adoniram was understandable. Their situations were eerily similar, both being outcasts of society. It angered Anna that tanners supplied the leather everyone used for their shoes, and even for the bags used for milk and wine, yet they were disparaged because of it. But then, no one had ever said that life was fair.

"Poor man," Leah whispered softly before shaking herself from her mental musings and hurrying to add the last few touches to an already-perfect feast.

When Levi and Adoniram returned to the triclinium much later, it was evident that the tanner had taken full advantage of the hot bath. Although the smell of the chemicals he used was imbedded in his skin, the full odor had been diminished by not only the bath and clean tunic, but by the scented lotion Magog had evidently given him to use.

For the first time since entering this house, Adoniram walked with his head held erect.

Everyone took their places on the reclining couches, including those servants who were followers of the Way. Those of Leah's servants who were devout Jews were here to serve the food to the guests, their day of worship having been yesterday's Sabbath.

Leah asked Levi to pray over the food. His words, so simple yet so heartfelt, brought a lump to Anna's throat. This is what she had missed the most, worshipping with other believers. Her father had refused to believe in Jesus as the Messiah and had forbidden Anna to do so, as well, but regardless of what he could do to inhibit her physically, he couldn't control her thoughts and her heart.

She had been secretly baptized in a mikvah in a believer's home when she had come to believe herself. Allowing Christ into her life had been the most wonderful thing that had ever happened to her. But that was the last time she had ever been able to attend a meeting of other worshippers. That is, until she had come here and found a precious sister in Leah.

When Levi proclaimed the bread as the body of Christ, the meal suddenly became more solemn. The loaf was passed around and everyone took a portion. Bowing her head, Anna focused on remembering the last time that Jesus had shared such a meal with his disciples, and the horrifying events that followed.

Levi then prayed over the wine. He held the goatskin bag aloft and squarely met the eyes of the tanner. The message that passed between them made Adoniram sit straighter as he realized what Levi was trying to say. *Jesus died for you, too. Everyone is precious in the Lord's sight.*

The look on Adoniram's face and the sheen of tears in his eyes brought a responsive wetness to Anna's eyes.

She recognized that look. It must have been the same one on her face when she had finally accepted that God truly loved her and wanted to be the Father she had never had.

The meal progressed uneventfully after that, though the mood in the room remained solemn.

Levi produced a scroll from the bag he had carried in with him, carefully unrolling it before him. He met the curious looks of all present with a smile.

"I have here a copy of a letter that the Apostle Paul wrote to the church in Corinth."

The room went from solemnity to excitement in a matter of seconds. The quietness of a moment before was shattered by the din that followed this announcement. Paul had written many letters, but they sometimes took years to make the rounds of the churches, if they made it at all. Such a gift was beyond anything they could have hoped for.

Levi raised his hand to bring silence then quietly read the scroll and, for the next several hours, it was discussed among them. The words that stuck with Anna the most she tried to embed in her memory by repeating them over and over.

"Praise be to the God and Father of our Lord Jesus Christ, the Father of compassion and the God of all comfort, who comforts us in all our troubles, so that we can comfort those in any trouble with the comfort we ourselves have received from God."

Father of compassion. The words swelled through her in a comforting wave. Her voice rang out loud and clear as they finished their worship with a song of praise.

Lucius passed through the gates of Jerusalem with a feeling akin to homecoming, something he had never felt before. He knew with keen insight that this feeling had more to do with Anna than anything else, but he couldn't for the life of him understand why. How had the woman so entrenched herself in his thoughts?

Thankfully, the rain that had been pelting them for the past two days had finally subsided, and the day proved to be much fairer than yesterday. The inclement weather had left his men in a morose mood, unlike him. The closer they got to Jerusalem, the more excited he became, despite being wet and muddy.

For the last several miles anticipation had been clawing at his insides, his restlessness communicating itself to his horse and making it skittish among the crowds. The horse's snorting and pawing sent people in the streets scattering out of his way, their surly looks of reproach following after them.

At the Antonia Fortress, Lucius handed his mount over to the waiting servants responsible for their care. He patted the horse's neck fondly, pulling a date from his pocket and smiling when the animal quickly snuffed it from his palm.

Andronicus joined him and they climbed the stairs to the fortress together.

"Do you intend to go see your mother?"

Surprised, Lucius turned to his companion. "Of course. Why do you ask?"

Andronicus shrugged. "I could use a decent meal myself."

Lucius stopped at the door, one eyebrow quirking upward. It was unusual for his friend to invite himself anywhere. The fact that he was avoiding Lucius's eyes provoked his suspicion.

"Why do I get the feeling there's more to this request than what you are saying?"

His friend colored in embarrassment, intriguing Lucius even more. A sudden thought occurred to Lucius and he paused, struggling with a feeling that was new to him, a fierce jealousy that made his insides twist in an uncomfortable way. Was Andronicus's sudden interest in his mother's home due to Anna's presence?

Andronicus opened the door and they passed through the entrance hall and into the open courtyard beyond. They walked in silence for several seconds before Lucius overcame his pique enough to speak.

"I'm certain my mother would welcome you."

Andronicus shook his head. "Maybe another time."

Angry with himself for his lack of hospitality, Lucius stopped the other man with a hand to his shoulder as he was about to walk away. "If I seemed less than enthusiastic, put it down to fatigue," he told him apologetically. "I would be pleased to have you go with me. It's been a long time since we've shared a meal together that wasn't army rations."

Andronicus hesitated. "Are you certain?"

"Of course."

Lucius didn't miss the lightening of Andronicus's face, and Lucius's smile faltered slightly as he once again wondered if the other man's reasons had anything to do with Anna.

"Give me a few minutes to clean up."

Nodding, Lucius agreed. "I need to do the same. I will meet you back here in half an hour."

Lucius and Andronicus separated, Lucius heading for the caldarium while Andronicus headed for the barracks.

Andronicus was waiting for him at the entrance a half hour later. The burning excitement in the other man's eyes registered a split second before Lucius noted that he had changed out of the short, blood-red tunic of the soldier and replaced it with a longer white one of the patrician. The toga that was wrapped around his body did nothing toward hiding the toned muscles that flexed whenever he moved.

Lucius felt again that niggle of jealousy that he had tried

to suppress earlier and realized that it had never been fully brought under subjection. Just whom was his bodyguard trying to impress anyway?

They left the Antonia behind them, both breathing a sigh of relief as they shook off thoughts of plots against the empire and putting down the rebellions that so infused this region. Their conversation centered on everyday things as they wound their way through the city's streets, but by silent mutual consent, they refrained from anything pertaining to war and politics. Tonight was a night to relax.

When they reached the villa, he recognized the serving girl who let them in. She was a tiny little thing, at least in comparison to Andronicus and himself, and rather plain of looks except for incredibly large, almond-shaped eyes that reminded him very much of Anna, yet without the same magnetic pull. Tapat was devoted to his mother, for which Lucius was grateful.

"Hello, Tapat. Will you tell my mother that I am here?"

She bobbed her head briefly, glancing at Andronicus before turning away.

Lucius looked at his friend also, surprised to see his gaze intently fixed on the retreating girl. The look on his face was hard to define. Lucius's dark brows winged upward. Perhaps it was not Anna who drew him here after all, leaving Lucius unsettled at the powerful feeling of relief that swept through him. Allowing himself to be involved with a Jew could only lead to trouble, yet no matter how hard he rebuked himself, he couldn't help the attraction he felt whenever he was anywhere near Anna.

Music from a lyre drifted out to them from the peristyle, followed by a voice that sounded so pure and sweet that he caught his breath at the beauty of it. They stopped, hesitant to intrude upon such a moment.

He and Andronicus stood unnoticed in the doorway,

watching Anna strumming the musical instrument with her eyes closed, the look of pure joy on her face impacting Lucius more than anything had in a very long time. What had been denied her in beauty was more than made up for in her golden voice.

Lucius stood transfixed, but then the words slowly penetrated his euphoria and caught his attention, making him frown.

"A Father to the fatherless, a defender of widows, is God in His holy dwelling."

If this God of theirs was a Father to the fatherless, He was doing a very poor job. And He also wasn't doing a very good job of defending Lucius's mother, who was a widow.

Tapat leaned down to Leah and indicated that the men were standing at the entrance to the peristyle. Leah came to her feet at once, causing Anna to break from her song. Anna's face colored crimson in embarrassment and she set the lyre aside. Lucius had to drag his eyes away from her to respond to his mother, who was at his side speaking to him.

"Lucius! Andronicus! You are just in time to share supper with us."

His mother's lilting voice did much to relieve some of the stress he had been under since their argument over the selling of the villa. It would seem she held no grudge after all, at least for now, but the situation was far from resolved. She had been unmoved by any of his arguments over her safety here in Jerusalem, and though he knew as *pater familias,* head of the family, he didn't need her permission to sell the villa or remove her to Rome, he didn't want to cause the breach between them that would ensue if he did so. He had one other weapon at his disposal, his mother's love for him, and he wouldn't hesitate to use it.

Smiling, Lucius bent to kiss her cheek. "That's what

we had hoped, Mother. Andronicus here is about to perish from lack of sustenance."

Andronicus acted as though he were about to melt away, pushing a hand through his dark brown hair and falling to his knees.

Leah laughed, shaking her head in friendly exasperation. "You know you are always welcome here, Andronicus, with or without your tribune."

Andronicus clutched her hand from where he knelt and held it to his lips.

"My lady, I will love you for eternity. You have surely saved my life!"

Lucius grinned at Andronicus's playacting. His bodyguard's lean, toned body and rippling muscles gave lie to the statement, for there was not another man under his command that could match Andronicus in size and power save Lucius himself.

"We were just about to have the meal brought in," she told them. "Please, take a seat."

The reclining couches could hold three normal-sized people, but since there was enough to go around they could each have their own. Lucius unobtrusively moved to take his position on the couch next to Anna.

She glanced up at him in surprise, quickly veiling her features, but not before he took note of the alarm in her eyes. His narrow-eyed gaze settled on her more firmly. Why was she so afraid of him? He had never threatened her in any way. In fact, he had been kindness itself. True, he was a Roman and she a Jew, but could it be something more elemental than that? Were the short breaths he could hear from fear, or something far different? He knew he should refrain from pursuing any such thought and just leave matters alone, but his ego wouldn't allow it.

"You have the most beautiful voice I have ever heard,"

he told her, and watched the color suffuse her face. He added to his mental inventory that she was unused to compliments, which only charmed him more.

"Thank you."

"The goddess Canens has certainly gifted you with such a golden voice."

Her soft brown eyes hardened to agate in an instant. "If my voice is a gift, it is a gift from Elohim, the Creator of the universe."

Surprised at her vehemence, it took him a moment to realize his offense. How could he have so forgotten that she was a Jew? Their refusal to believe in other gods had given them the reputation of being atheists and had set much of Rome against them. As for himself, since he didn't believe in *anything,* he didn't really care.

"I meant no offense, I assure you. It was intended as a compliment."

She relaxed back against the couch she was reclining on, studying him warily, as though he were a cobra about to strike.

Trying to make amends, he gave her his most persuasive smile. "Who taught you to play the lyre?"

She glanced down at the instrument, her fingers gliding over it almost lovingly. "My mother gave me a lyre when I was small, but she died before she could teach me to play."

Her face saddened at some remembered thought. "I taught myself to play."

It didn't take a prophet to realize that she would have done so during many lonely hours. He was glad that his mother had the instrument for her to use. Thinking to remove the sadness from her expression, he told her, "Perhaps you would sing again after the meal?"

Her look of horror amused him. Problems be hanged,

he was going to enjoy watching this flower open up under his tutelage.

He settled back on his couch, reaching for the succulent pheasant on the tray on the table before him. Giving Anna his most compelling look, he handed her a piece of the fowl. She reluctantly took it from him, refusing to meet his eyes.

Tapat filled his goblet with wine and Lucius thanked her, noting Andronicus's watchful regard of the servant. She in turn ignored his bodyguard. Intriguing.

They were halfway through the meal when his mother suddenly grabbed her chest, moaned and collapsed on her couch.

Chapter 8

Anna watched from her seat by the atrium's pool as Lucius paced up and down like a caged lion, his hobnailed sandals tapping against the marble tiles in an unending, monotonous rhythm. Every few minutes, he went to the bottom of the stairway that led to the upper floor and stared upward. Shoving his dark hair back with a shaking hand, he would then resume his pacing.

While Lucius had sent for the Roman doctor who tended to the troops, Anna had secretly sent Tapat and Michael to find Levi and bring him here. But, whereas the Roman doctor was close by at the Antonia, it would take some time for Levi to arrive.

Phlegon was upstairs examining Leah now and he had asked that everyone leave the room to afford them privacy. Anna didn't trust the physician, but she would give him the benefit of the doubt. He must surely know something about medicine, even if he didn't know the true God who had created it. At least that was her very fervent hope.

Ever since Leah's collapse, Anna had sent up an unceasing petition for her recovery. How much time had passed she wasn't certain, but it seemed like hours since that fateful moment.

"Andronicus."

Anna started as Lucius's firm voice interrupted the silent pall that had settled over the room.

Andronicus stepped forward, his anxious gaze probing his superior. It had surprised Anna that he appeared to be as rattled as Lucius. It had also impressed her that he had refused to leave his side, his loyalty and friendship unquestionable.

Lucius gripped his shoulder. "Go to the commander. Let him know what has happened. Tell him that I will be staying here for the foreseeable future."

Although Andronicus was not in his uniform, he nonetheless slammed his right fist against his chest in salutation. Nodding his head, he moved to leave but then stopped at the door. He turned back to Lucius.

"You will let me know when you find out anything?"

Their eyes met and a message passed between them that Anna couldn't hope to interpret.

"I will," Lucius agreed.

Andronicus's lips pressed together, his face wreathed in silent commiseration. He glanced briefly at Anna and then exited.

Anna caught Lucius's look and gave him a tentative smile. She would like nothing more right now than to go to him and wrap him in her arms and try to soothe that look of agony from his face. If only she could assure him that Leah was in Elohim's hands, but even Leah hesitated to talk about the one true God around her son. Yet, surely it was the very thing that would give him the most comfort at this time.

He came and sat next to her on the edge of the atrium's pool. He placed his elbows against his bent knees and shoved his palms back through his hair, hiding his face from her view. He said nothing, his anguish communicated by the depth of his silence.

Even if he were a believer, Anna wouldn't know what to say to assuage his fear and grief. Instead, she broke several Jewish laws by placing her hand against his back in quiet sympathy. He turned his head slightly, meeting her eyes, and something happened in that moment that she could never afterward explain. The only way to describe it would be to say that it was a convergence of their destinies, some instinct that told her that from this moment on, their lives would be forever connected in some way. The odd feeling of insight left her feeling more confused than ever.

She quickly removed her hand, pulling her eyes away from his. Before either one could speak, the door to his mother's room opened. Lucius was on his feet in an instant, striding to the stairs and taking them two at a time.

Anna heard him ask after his mother, but then their voices became too low to hear anything further. She rose to her feet, intent on finding out Leah's condition, but the two men went inside the bedroom and shut the door firmly behind them.

Left to her own devices, Anna went into the triclinium to help clear the room of the meal that had been abandoned so hurriedly, but the servants, under Magog's supervision, had already put the room to rights. Not knowing what else to do, she returned to the atrium to await further news.

The time dragged unendingly. Restless, Anna got up and went into the peristyle, hoping some of the peace that she normally felt while in the outdoor garden would settle her raw nerves.

The garden was alive with spring and the beauty that the spring rains always brought. Bougainvillea vines spread their bright pink blossoms everywhere, as did the flowering fruit trees. The scent of acacia blossoms filled the air, while a pair of doves cooed to each other from the top of a flowering myrtle tree. Life seemed to be flourishing everywhere, except in the room upstairs.

Anna sat down on the bench near the fountain in the center of the peristyle. The water spraying from the mouths of the two twining stone fish gave a soothing cadence that never failed to calm her. Even now she felt herself relax enough to allow her to pray for God's will to be done.

It was a hard thing to do. Everything in her wanted to storm at Elohim to spare Leah's life. She had grown to love the woman as though she were her own mother. If her heart was being torn apart at the thought of her death, what must it be like for her only son?

"Anna?"

Anna jumped, startled by Lucius's sudden appearance. So deep in thought and prayer had she been, she had not even heard him enter the garden. She rose quickly to her feet, almost afraid to ask.

"Your mother?"

"Still alive, but barely."

His voice was close to desperation.

"Is there anything that I can do?"

He stared at her unblinkingly and she grew uncomfortable under his regard.

"How do I reach this God of yours? What do I have to do to get Him to let my mother live?"

Anna didn't know whether to be appalled or delighted. The fact that he didn't deny the existence of the true God gave her hope, but how was she to put into plain words Elohim's great love when his pagan mind was used to demanding sacrifices? She felt decidedly inadequate to explain such things to him.

"You can't bargain with God," she told him quietly.

The anger that seemed always so close to the surface sparked in his eyes. Jerking a flower from the bush beside him, he crushed it in his fist.

"Why would your God do this to her when she loves and serves Him? What kind of Father is that?"

Anna wanted to turn away from his accusing stare, but she was caught by the apprehension in his face. This, then, was the major crux of the problem. Lucius was seeing God through the eyes of an angry child who had been betrayed by his own earthly father. How was she to explain God's purpose to him when he couldn't see past his own pain? Her empathetic observance came from her own experience with a similar pain.

"Every moment of every life is a strand in the tapestry of God's design," she told him softly. "Everything He does works for the good of those who love Him and have been called according to His purpose. He is God, Lucius, not just our heavenly Father."

Magog interrupted them before Lucius could say something vitriolic that she was sure he would regret later.

"Master, your grandfather is here."

Anna noted the rapid rising and falling of Lucius's chest hinting at his agitation. His eyes glittered with pain and rage.

"If your God takes my mother, I promise you, I will make war on Him myself."

He strode from the room, leaving Anna frozen with a terrifying fear for him.

* * *

Lucius watched Levi ministering to Leah with a wary eye and no little amount of trepidation. The man had come unleashed on Lucius when he had seen the bowl of leeches gorged with Leah's blood. For an old man, he hadn't lost any of his ability to speak forcefully.

Lucius's ears were still ringing with words about life being in the blood and sucking the life out of a person, and something to do with heathen ignorance. Funny how each physician considered the other a heathen.

Anna entered the room, and Lucius immediately felt her presence with every fiber of his being. Their eyes met briefly before she turned hurriedly away. He knew that he had hurt her with his last statement, but he had meant every word. He had mentally shaken his fist at her God.

Anna handed Levi the brew that had been concocted in the kitchen from the supplies Levi had brought with him. Lucius stepped forward, intent on intervening, but then hesitated. He was willing to try anything at this point if it would help his mother.

"What did your Roman physician tell you?" Levi asked absently as he stirred the contents of the cup.

Lucius glanced at Levi skeptically, reluctant to offer the other physician's explanation. If the leeches had set the man off, he was fairly certain that Phlegon's words would bring forth an acerbic tirade without end.

"He said the gods were against her."

Levi turned to him angrily, his mouth open to deliver a telling lecture. Lucius held up his palms. "I don't believe it, either." But neither did he hold their Jewish God unaccountable, if there was such a god. He had been on too many campaigns and seen too many gods to trust in any one, despite his mother's admonitions to the contrary during his childhood years.

With a final glare in Lucius's direction, Levi relaxed back on the stool and started spooning some of the contents of the bowl into Leah's mouth, using his fingers to gently massage her neck to make her swallow. One side of her mouth refused to move, as did one side of her body, but her eyes shot sparks of fire. Her words came out slurred but understandable.

"Don' tak 'bout me like em na her."

Levi had the audacity to grin at her. "I'm not certain if the mandragora that heathen gave you is working, or if your lack of speech is due to your illness, or both, but it's nice to see that you haven't lost your spirit."

Lucius grew irritated at his attempt at levity. "What do you say is wrong with her?"

Levi became solemn. "From the symptoms I have noticed over the last few weeks, I would say it has something to do with her heart. But unlike your Roman physicians, Jews do not believe in vivisection, nor desecrating a body, so our knowledge is not as...precise as yours. I can only speculate from having witnessed such symptoms before."

Lucius glanced from him to his mother. "What was that concoction you just gave her for?"

Gathering up his supplies, Levi handed them to Anna before answering.

"It's a willow bark tea. For some reason, it seems to lessen the pain and many of the symptoms in such cases. The mandragora will put her to sleep, but the willow bark will lessen the severity of the attack."

That, at least, was somewhat reassuring. "Will she be all right?"

Levi looked at Lucius, his countenance grim, then he turned and stared hard into Leah's eyes. "You knew, didn't you?"

It was a moment before Leah nodded.

Lucius glared from one to the other. "Knew what?"

"That it's only a matter of time," Levi answered. The smile he gave his daughter was a sad one. "It's why you wanted me to come, isn't it?"

Again, Leah nodded. She grasped Anna's hand with the hand that was unaffected by the paralysis. The look she gave her father was fierce. "From God."

Anna sat down next to her on the bed and squeezed her hand. The two women stared at each other in silent understanding, leaving Lucius isolated from their camaraderie. They had a communication that transcended words and Lucius was surprised to find himself envious of that bond.

Anna gently pushed the hair away from his mother's face and his mother sighed. He watched as the mandragora drug took effect and her lashes slowly drifted downward. Both physicians had put her fate into the hands of unseen beings that were ready to send her to the hereafter.

He couldn't accept their ready resignation of such a prognosis, however. Since Phlegon was an old-school physician, and Levi, by his own words, was lacking in knowledge, Lucius knew what he must do. He had to get his mother to Rome as soon as possible. He knew other physicians who had a more modern and complete understanding of the human body. There had to be something that could be done. He wasn't about to lose his mother.

He moved to the door, casting Anna and Levi a commanding look.

"I need to speak with you."

Tapat took Anna's place next to Leah, the tearstains on her face an indication of a recent weep. Satisfied that his mother was being watched, Lucius motioned with his head that the others were to follow him.

* * *

Levi followed Lucius from the room, Anna close behind them. Lucius waited for them to exit before closing the door. He descended the stairs, his tense posture warning Anna that whatever he had on his mind was very serious and probably about to change her life again.

Lucius stopped in the atrium and turned to them, his shoulders set in an uncompromising line.

"I'm taking my mother to Rome."

Anna felt her heart drop in panic, her mind going blank as she tried to come to terms with all the implications of that one statement.

Levi was the one who answered him. "To move her now would be dangerous."

Lucius studied his grandfather, several thoughts flitting across his face. That he didn't trust Levi was obvious.

"You say she has only a matter of time. How long?"

Sighing, Levi shook his head hopelessly. "Only Elohim knows that. It could be days. It could be weeks, maybe even years."

The room settled into silence for several heartbeats. Anna watched Lucius struggle with his decision on what was best for his mother, his mouth finally pressing into a grim line.

"I have decided. We are going to Rome. I will make certain that she is well cared for and protected from the elements."

He turned to Anna and she felt the full force of his persuasive personality in the look he gave her.

"I want you to come too."

Astonishment gave way to pure horror. Did he even have any idea what he was suggesting? A Christian in Rome would be fair game for the enemies of Christ who were trying to annihilate them. And that included his mother.

But, then, was it truly any better for them here in Jerusalem? Christians seemed to be hated everywhere. But, at least this was home.

She slowly shook her head. "I cannot."

Lucius's eyes darkened with animosity. "You would desert my mother after all she has done for you?"

"That's unfair, Lucius," Levi objected heatedly. "You have no idea what you are asking of her."

"I have every idea. I'm asking her to give my mother the same courtesy that was given to her when she had nowhere to go and no one to rely on."

"She has Tapat," Anna remonstrated, not wanting to usurp the other woman in Leah's affections. Anna was very fond of Tapat and wouldn't hurt her for the world.

Anna couldn't understand the look that passed across Lucius's face.

"Tapat can't go. She needs to stay here. She has…obligations."

What obligations could the other woman have that would preclude her from leaving Jerusalem? The glare Lucius gave her warned her not to ask. But, if what he said was true, there was no way Anna could allow Leah to go to Rome on her own, especially not in her condition. Swallowing hard, she nodded her head slightly.

"I will go."

Lucius released his breath, closing his eyes briefly. "Thank you."

Levi interrupted. "And if your mother refuses to go?"

Anna didn't like the smile that graced Lucius's face. It hinted at a ruthlessness she had yet to encounter in him, reminding her again that he was very much a Roman.

"Leave my mother to me."

Thinking she understood Levi's objections, she told him, "You could come, as well."

He shook his head, his long, gray sideburns swaying from side to side. "No, my place is here. This is the place where my Lord walked for so long. I feel an affinity for Him here."

Anna understood. Despite her hard life, she loved Judea. The desert spoke to her in ways that a Roman coming from the green and fertile land of Italy couldn't possibly understand.

Lucius glanced from one to the other. "I will see about making arrangements for this house to sell and for immediate transportation to Caesarea Maritima." He took Anna by the arm. "I will be at the Antonia. If anything happens to my mother, send for me at once."

Anna nodded her head and watched him until he exited through the door. She turned to Levi and found him watching her instead, one eyebrow lifted, but he said nothing.

Coloring hotly, she wondered if the feelings that had suddenly descended upon her had been visible on her face. How was it possible to have such strong feelings for a man she had known for such a short time? Her feelings of gratitude had subtly evolved into something much stronger and much more confusing.

Levi stroked his beard thoughtfully, staring up at Leah's room. "I suppose I should go and pave the way for Lucius's return."

"What is it that concerns you most, Levi?" Anna asked, realizing that something serious was on the old man's mind.

Levi sighed heavily. "If she really doesn't want to go to Rome, I'm afraid the worry could kill her more quickly than staying here."

Anna set her shoulders resolutely. "Then we need to pray before we do anything."

Levi acted as though he hadn't heard her. "My daughter will be walking into the very heart of Satan's domain," he mumbled, his shoulders sagging wearily. "I will never see her again."

Touched by his misery, Anna laid a hand on his shoulder. "You never know," she disagreed.

When he turned to her, Anna felt herself go cold all over. His eyes were glassy and his voice sounded hollow, like a temple priest who had just come from the Holy of Holies.

"The beginning of birth pains."

Chapter 9

Lucius watched a cargo ship glide through the stone column entrance of the port of Caesarea, awed by the marvel of man-made engineering that had been commissioned by King Herod many years ago.

Herod had named the port city for his friend Augustus, and it was Jewish only in location. The spirit of this city was Roman, as were most of the buildings and trade, allowing Lucius to relax his guard for the first time since he had entered Israel. This city was like a miniature Rome, and he felt more at home here than anywhere in this wretched country.

The harbor was lined with buildings of white marble and limestone, their walls glistening in the bright sunlight. Several ships were anchored here, workers busily scurrying about with amphorae of wine and salt, baskets of grain and a host of other supplies waiting to be loaded onto them.

Several merchants had set up tents on the stone walkways to do their work out of the sun.

Lucius made his way to a Roman galley anchored close by. A new group of legionnaires had debarked only this morning and would be replacing Lucius's group. The waiting ship would then take him, his family and his troops back to Rome.

Some unseen hand had provided the means by which he could leave Judea and return to his homeland. As he had been looking into a way to sell his mother's villa, a post had arrived recalling his group to Rome. A new general would be taking over, one who was much more rigid than his predecessor. With tensions rising here and the threat of revolt a very real possibility, Rome was taking no chances.

At the same time, one of the centurions stationed at the Antonia had mentioned to Lucius that he was looking for a villa in the upper city. In moments, a deal had been brokered and Lucius was free of any hindrances that might keep him here.

Lucius walked up the gangplank that was still attached to the dock and met Andronicus at the top. He glanced quickly around at the hive of activity on the ship.

"Has everything been made ready?"

Andronicus nodded, a sardonic grin splitting his face. "Aye. Your cabin has been remade into a luxurious harem."

Lucius gave him a look that warned him that his attempt at humor was not appreciated, and Andronicus laughed, not at all disturbed by his superior's vexation.

"It has been made comfortable," he amended, still grinning.

"I only hope I'm not making a mistake," Lucius told him, his brows drawing down into a frown. "I will never forgive myself if something happens to my mother on this trip."

Andronicus turned serious. "You are certain she was not poisoned?"

Lucius watched a stuppator caulking the sides of the ship, his agile movements while hanging from a rope speaking of many years' experience. "At this point, I'm not certain of anything." He glanced back at his bodyguard. "But it seems highly unlikely. Apparently my mother has had a condition for some time that she failed to apprise me of."

"I'm sorry."

Lucius recognized his condolences with a slight nod. "Let me check with the captain and I will let you know when we can leave. It will probably be several days, so take advantage of the entertainments here if you would like."

"I might do that. There's a chariot race at the Hippodrome today I would like to see."

It had been some time since Lucius had been to a race. "I might join you."

Perhaps he could persuade Anna to attend with him. He was fairly certain that she had never seen a chariot race before, but would she like it?

He parted from Andronicus wondering why he should even care.

Anna got up from her seat next to Leah's bed, brushed back the graying hair from her sleeping face and quietly walked out onto the balcony of the villa Lucius had brought them to. The house was owned by a friend of Lucius and he had welcomed them, literally, with open arms.

Leah was doing much better, although her body was still half paralyzed. The frustration with her condition was evident in her dark eyes, but she never complained. Her speech was still slurred due to the paralysis on the left side of her face, but it was still understandable, at least more so now than in the beginning. She slept a lot, leaving Anna with a great deal of time on her hands.

The Great Sea was visible in the distance, as was the busy harbor. Anna had never seen anything like it in her life. Never having been farther from her home in Bethany than Jerusalem, she had always thought that nothing could ever compare in beauty to Jerusalem, but she knew now that she was mistaken.

This city was a glittering testament to Herod's love of wealth. It was now Palestine's major seaport and had been created, literally, out of the sand. Not being close to a freshwater source, the huge aqueducts in the distance were built to bring water from Mount Carmel nearly ten miles away. They spanned the desert sand for as far as the eye could see. No expense had been spared to make this city as much like Rome as possible.

The thought brought her no pleasure. Here among all this wealth and beauty were dozens of statues and temples to the various gods the Romans favored. If this city was only a speck compared to the great Rome, as Lucius had told her, her heart quailed at the thought of the paganism she was about to live among.

Noise from the courtyard below caught her attention. Three children, two boys and a girl, were chasing a small wooden ball around the yard. Anna recognized them as the children of the owner. The girl's name was Cara, the oldest boy Cassius and the youngest Flavius. They were all under the age of ten with the girl being the youngest.

Their laughter and squeals brought a quick smile to Anna's face. Children were the same everywhere. Wasn't that why the Lord had said that the kingdom of heaven was for such as them? Their uninhibited joy, their innocence. If she stretched past the pain in her memory, she could remember such a time herself.

Cara stopped suddenly, her eyes widening with delight at something just beyond Anna's vision. With a scream, she ran forward, dark hair flying out behind her, and met the man who was just coming into Anna's sight. He lifted the child in his arms, hugging her fiercely and bringing on a fit of giggles from the girl.

Anna recognized the man now. Petronius. He was the child's father and the owner of this villa. His purple-trimmed toga showed that he had access to the Imperial Senate, yet Anna found him to be surprisingly spontaneous and friendly. Her perception of Romans had been colored by the only ones she had ever known, soldiers of the Roman army sent to bring her people into subjection, men like Lucius who had lost their ability to see past their orders.

But then, that wasn't exactly true either. What she had seen of Lucius in the past two weeks had altered her opinion of him greatly. His gentleness and care for his mother had impressed her considerably. No expense was spared in giving her comfort on this journey, and that care had been extended to Anna, as well. No, Lucius was a man like none she had ever encountered.

Petronius carried his daughter over and joined his sons, who were quietly awaiting him. Petronius turned Cara until she was able to cling to his back. He then grabbed the ball Flavius was holding and threw it on the ground, kicking it with his foot.

Cara screamed encouragement as the boys immediately joined in the game of keep-away.

Petronius was a good father. It was obvious that he adored his wife and children.

A sad smile tilted Anna's lips. What would her life have been like with such a father? She would never know.

Watching the children brought on a mood of melancholy. As for herself, she had given up long ago on the idea of marriage, but, oh, how she longed to have children and a home of her own.

Perhaps in Rome she would find a man who would look past her plain appearance and lack of dowry but, after all she had been taught to believe, could she possibly marry a Gentile even if he was a Christian?

Lately, whenever she tried to picture herself married, the tribune's face seemed to hover in her mind. It bothered her a lot that she couldn't banish the man from her thoughts, especially since he was not a believer.

As though her reflections had conjured him, he walked into his mother's room. Glancing at her sleeping form, he changed course and made his way to where Anna stood watching him guardedly.

She could remember only one time when she had seen him out of uniform. Lucius's formidable looks gave him the appearance of a man to be reckoned with, as she had already found out was true.

Facing her, he leaned one arm against the balcony and glanced over at the garden. "What are you looking at?"

He was too close for her peace of mind. Her heart's tempo increased to a fevered pitch, her palms growing sweaty. She followed his look and realized the peristyle was now empty. "I was watching Petronius playing with his children," she told him, moving slightly away from him to put more space between them. "He's a very loving father."

Lucius's smile lacked humor. "Something you and I would know nothing about."

Their eyes met and she could see the gleam in his that told her he had noticed her withdrawal from him. A warm spring breeze blew inward from the sea, molding her soft blue tunic against her and his look changed instantly to one she couldn't interpret. She quickly turned away.

"Perhaps that is so, but it is good to know that there are

fathers who are not like ours." She leaned both forearms against the balcony, watching the birds playing in the garden's fountain spray. "Loving fathers. Just like Elohim."

Anna wasn't looking at Lucius, but she felt him tense. She glanced his way and saw that any trace of humor had fled.

"This Father God of yours who let His Son die on a cross, who allowed you to be abused, who is allowing my mother to die?" he asked coldly.

Sighing, Anna asked him a question in return. "Did your mother ever ask you not to do something that you did anyway?"

His narrow-eyed gaze clashed with hers. "Of course. What has that to do with anything?"

"Your mother told me that when you were a small child she would tell you stories from the scriptures before you went to sleep at night. I know you are aware of the creation story, so you know that Elohim created a perfect world free of evil and sin. It was mankind that destroyed that." She turned away again, unable to face his determined opinion. "It would be useless to argue that with you when you know it to be true."

"So it's our free will that causes all the evil in the world?"

He moved closer and this time it was she who tensed. She kept her gaze fixed firmly on the ships moving in and out of the harbor in the distance. He moved her hair from in front of her shoulder to behind it, and she caught her breath.

"What of your life of brutality?" he asked her, his voice growing husky and sending alarm ringing through her mind. "Why should you be punished for something you had no control over?"

It took a great effort on her part to be able to look him in the face again, and this time, there was no looking away. She was caught by the intensity of his expression.

"If not for my father," she told him softly, her own voice becoming huskier, "your mother and grandfather would never have been reunited. There is a purpose for everything, Tribune."

"Lucius."

She frowned. "What?"

"I am not your tribune and you are not a soldier. My name is Lucius."

She wanted to look away, but a will stronger than her own wouldn't allow it. "I am only a servant," she told him firmly.

The darkening of his eyes warned of a rising temper. "Has anyone suggested such to you?"

She frowned again. "Well…no…but…"

He stopped her with a finger to her lips. Cupping her cheek with his palm, he moved even closer and Anna found it hard to breathe.

"You are no servant, Anna," he told her, his eyes intense. "You are my mother's friend and, therefore, my friend, as well."

They stared into each other's eyes for some time until a movement from inside the bedroom caught their attention. Leah was awake.

Lucius leaned back against the concrete step behind him and watched Anna in amusement. She sat next to him twisting the belt hanging around her waist until it was knotted so much he doubted she would ever unravel it.

He had brought her with him to the Hippodrome to watch the chariot race scheduled for today, although it had taken a lot of persuasion on his part to get her here. It was patently obvious that she didn't want to be here, but just as obvious that she was reluctantly enthralled.

He had chosen seats three rows above the interior wall

that protected spectators from the animals that were often brought in for amusement. The frescoes of plants and animals were innocuous enough, but she wrinkled her cute little nose at the paintings of the gladiators.

The sea beyond the stadium was rushing against the shore, its soothing rhythm slowly disappearing under the sounds of the increasing crowds.

"I shouldn't be here."

He glanced down at her and was suddenly sorry that they had come. He didn't want to undo all the inroads he had made toward gaining her trust.

"It's just a chariot race."

That was certainly true enough. He only hoped her Jewish prudishness wouldn't be offended by the opening ceremonies.

Andronicus joined them, nodding at Lucius and smiling at Anna. He searched the arena for a particular chariot whose colors were well known by everyone who enjoyed the games.

"I heard that Quintas will be racing today."

"I heard the same," Lucius agreed, joining in the hunt. "Do you see him?"

"There he is!" The enthusiasm in Andronicus's voice invoked an equal excitation in Lucius. "In the green. Secundus is in red."

"It should be a good contest," Lucius remarked as the other charioteers lined up.

He glanced again at Anna and noticed her chewing on her bottom lip. He decided to try to put her at ease by engaging her in conversation and keeping her attention away from the half-clad dancers gyrating around the arena.

"So you've never seen a chariot race?"

She shook her head slightly.

He continued to watch her, noting the color blooming in

her cheeks as he did so. Was she remembering their time on the balcony as he was? It had been the only thing on his mind for the last several hours. He had come close to taking her up on the unintentional invitation he had seen in her guileless eyes, but he knew that would have surely destroyed what little faith she had in him. But it had been a battle to bring into subjection the intense feelings she had invoked in him at that particular moment.

What was it exactly that fascinated him so about her? She wasn't pretty, but her skin was like smooth marble, and the desire to touch it was a temptation he had been fighting for some time now.

And those eyes of hers. He was bewitched by the paradox of innocence that at the same time allured. It had been a long time since he had seen such purity in a woman, something many men in Rome would pay a high price for.

Trumpets announced the beginning of the race. Andronicus leaned forward, excitement glittering in his eyes.

They all turned to watch the chariots get into their final positions. Even with the screams and excitement all around him, Lucius found it hard to take his eyes off Anna. He was more interested in watching her expression than in the race, and right now that expression was one of awed fascination with the beauty of the horses stamping and pawing the dirt in the arena.

The charioteers slowly began making their first round of the arena behind the flag bearers. The crowd cheered them on, everyone yelling for their favorites.

When Quintas passed in front of them, Andronicus leapt to his feet, cheering enthusiastically. Lucius had to grin at the disconcerted look Anna gave Andronicus before turning a questioning one to him. He just shook his head. She would have to wait to see what made crowds of people willing to sit for quite some time in the hot sun eating the dust flung from flying hooves.

He bent closer so that she could hear him. "Which one would you choose?"

She studied the horses again. "The golden ones with the cream-colored manes and tails."

Lucius smiled. "You have a good eye. They are a matched pair and belong to Petronius, by the way."

She turned sharply to face him, her features going from surprise to delight. "Then I will cheer for them."

"Shall I make a wager for you?"

She shook her head adamantly, and shrugging, he settled back in his seat to watch as the charioteers reached the end of the arena and prepared for the race.

The crowd grew quiet when the proconsul rose from his seat and dedicated the race to Caesar.

Anna turned to Lucius and it was the first time he had ever seen such intense anger on her face. Perhaps he shouldn't have brought her here, but he thought it best to have her Romanized as soon as possible before they actually reached the great city, and the chariot races were the least offensive sport. Many Jews attended the races.

Anna's unfriendly look settled on him and he felt a prism of guilt, but at what exactly, he wasn't quite certain. Living in Rome, she was going to have to get used to hearing Caesar's name wherever she went.

The starting flags dropped and the race began. The crowd came to their feet, roaring their approval. There would be eight rounds to the finish, yet of the ten charioteers, it would be unusual if more than five survived to the finish. Remembering past races, Lucius really began to worry that he shouldn't have brought Anna here.

After three rounds without mishap, Lucius began to relax. Anna was cheering as enthusiastically as the rest of the crowd. She and Andronicus were trying to outdo each other in their encouragement of the charioteer they had chosen. Regardless of his friendship with Petronius, Andronicus favored Quintas, as did most of the mob.

At the fifth round, one chariot pushed another into the wall, causing it to flip and crash. The crowd cheered wildly, but Anna stared horrified at the people around her. She settled back into her seat, no longer interested in the race. She was watching as arena slaves hurried to remove the debris and the injured man. She closed her eyes, her mouth moving silently and Lucius realized that she was praying for the injured man. He glanced uncomfortably around at the surrounding crowd, but no one was paying attention.

The other racers were coming around the end of the track at breakneck speed. The slaves who were trying to remove the debris from the other chariot were having a problem. It was soon obvious that they would never get the broken chariot out of the way in time. The closest charioteer realized it at the last minute and tried to move his horses out of the way. Although the horses cleared the overturned vehicle, the chariot did not and its wheel caught. At the speed he had been going, the wheel of his chariot broke off and began bouncing across the track. It hit a piece of the overturned chariot and bounced into the air.

Lucius saw what was about to happen and knew he had no way to prevent it. With lightning reflexes, he pushed Anna to the floor and wrapped his body around her. The wheel slammed against his back, pushing the breath from his body in a long whoosh.

Chapter 10

For a brief instant, all sound receded into the background. Lucius shook his head, seeking to hold off the darkness that was trying to take him down. He could hear, as though from a distance, Andronicus's panicked voice calling his name, and then the sound rushed back in upon him in a frenzy.

Slowly lifting himself onto his forearms, he anxiously studied the woman beneath him. Her eyes were huge in a face made white by alarm. With a trembling hand, he gently pushed the hair out of her face.

"Are you all right?"

Lucius was still shaken. He had never been so afraid in his life. In the split second it took to realize that Anna would be killed, he knew that she had become too important to him for him to lose her.

Taking a deep breath, she nodded. "I am well. And you?"

Lucius pushed himself to his feet, flinching as the

pain in his back brought on another wave of dizziness. He reached down and helped Anna to her feet. She adjusted her tunic, which had become skewed, brushing off the dirt and sand.

"I am just a little bruised. Nothing to worry about," he told her.

"Tribune!"

Lucius glanced at his bodyguard and noticed that his face was as white as the marble columns of the Hippodrome.

"I am well, Andronicus."

Andronicus blew out a slow breath as his tense body visibly relaxed.

Lucius took note of the damage around him. He and Anna had been lucky. Two others had not. They lay crushed beneath the wheel, which had bounced off his back and landed on them. Several slaves were moving through the crowd to reach them and remove the bodies. Only those people closest to them gave them any notice. Everyone else was still busy cheering on the charioteers. He should have been amazed at their lack of concern, but he was not. It was the way of the people.

As for him, the race no longer held any appeal nor, he suspected, for Anna, as well. He took the shawl she was shaking out and helped her to situate it around her head and shoulders. Placing his palms on each side of her face, he quietly studied her.

"You are certain you are all right?" he asked, his heart rate only now beginning to subside. When she nodded, he told her, "Then let us go home."

Anna sat at Leah's bedside watching her sleep, a worried frown marring her face. Leah appeared to be growing weaker but Lucius didn't seem to notice, or if he did, he attributed it to a different cause than what Anna suspected.

Lucius believed that the physicians in Rome could help his ailing mother. What he didn't understand was the attachment the Jews had for their homeland. They drew their very life from the soil and the air that they breathed. It was an attitude that Rome had never understood.

Leah obediently followed where her son wanted to lead, but it was a terrible wrench having to choose between leaving her home and, most especially, her father or leaving her son.

For Anna there had been no choice. She owed this woman and her son her life. She would never be able to repay them for what they had done. And if that wasn't enough reason to follow them into the very heart of paganism, her love for both of them was.

She watched two doves on the balcony without really seeing them. Her mind was caught up in the wonder of her discovery.

She frowned. Was she merely grateful for the kindness that had been shown to her, for Lucius having saved her life twice now? Since she had never been in love, she had no way of knowing if these feelings were of a lasting nature.

Whenever Lucius looked in her eyes the way he had at the arena today, her heart raced faster than the speeding chariots. When he touched her, heat coursed through her. But these were mere physical signs of something she had yet to understand. How did one know when it was really love?

Lucius strode into the room, his countenance darkening with worry when he took note of his mother's white face.

"How is she?"

At the sign of his distress, Anna forgot her own worries. He needed her reassurance, not her uncertainty.

"She is a little better today, I think. She had a good night."

He carefully settled himself on the bed next to Leah so as not to awaken her, his face softened with his love.

"I can't lose her."

Anna's heart broke for him. She knew what it was like to lose a beloved mother. Before she could respond, Leah's eyes fluttered open and she stared hard at her son. "We all have to die sometime."

Various expressions chased themselves across Lucius's face—surprise, fear, love. He cupped one of her hands in his as though he could pass some of his strength on to her.

"Not you. Not now. I need you too much."

"Elohim decides the hours of our life. If it is my time to go, then nothing you can do will stop it."

"Mother," Lucius told her quietly, "do you not know that my life would be a wasteland without you?"

Leah's lips turned down into a frown, the paralyzed side of her face making her look somewhat grotesque. "I have been a stumbling block to you."

Lucius scowled. "How so?"

Releasing his hand, Leah adjusted herself on the pillow until she was sitting up.

"I should never have allowed myself to force you to replace your father's spot in my life."

"What are you talking about?" Lucius visibly tensed at her admonition.

"You should have a wife and a family by now, not be waiting on a selfish mother."

Anna thought it time for her to leave the room. She moved to do so, but Leah held out her hand.

"No, Anna, don't go. We are finished."

Eyebrows flying upward, Lucius told her, "We most certainly are not finished."

"Well, I am." Leah pushed at Lucius to make him get off the bed. "I have rested enough, now let me up. It is almost time for supper and I, for one, am starving."

Anna hid a grin at Leah's returning spirit and Lucius's helplessness in the face of it. Leah's body might be growing weaker, but there was certainly nothing wrong with her tongue.

Heaving a protracted sigh, Lucius gave way, but his look warned that their discussion was not at an end. Leah chose to ignore him. When she leaned against his shoulder for support, she noticed his wince of pain.

"You are hurt?"

Neither Lucius nor Anna had apprised her of the afternoon's events. Their eyes met over Leah's head and Lucius shook his head ever so slightly in caution.

"It is nothing. I am fine."

Leah glanced from one to the other, her eyes narrowing in speculation. "Tell me."

"Mother…"

"Tell me."

Mother and son glared at each other for several long seconds, two powerful wills facing off against each other. Lucius was the first one to give way.

"Fine, I will tell you, but will you please sit back down?"

Leah did as asked, waiting for an explanation.

"It was just a little accident."

Anna made a slight noise of protest and they both turned her way. She dropped her eyes to the floor, afraid that Leah would be able to read into them her horror of that afternoon. Even now, she could feel the color draining from her face at the memory.

"Perhaps Anna should tell me," Leah suggested drily.

Before she could do so, Lucius told her, "We went to the chariot races and there was a slight accident."

"How slight?"

Anna interrupted. "The tribune saved my life."

She hadn't meant to let that slip out, and from Lucius's glare he certainly didn't appreciate it. There was nothing to do now but fill his mother in on the details, though he did it in such a way as to relieve her of any worry. Still, his mother read between the lines, hearing more from what he didn't say than from what he did.

Anna was glad Leah was sitting down when she saw her waxen color.

"We are fine, Mother," Lucius assured her.

Leah slowly rose to her feet. "Sit down and let me look at your back."

"It is nothing, I tell you."

Again, that face-off of wills. It was clear from whom Lucius had derived his stubbornness. Rolling his eyes upward, Lucius sat.

Leah tugged down the back of his tunic, sucking in a sharp breath at what she saw. Curious, Anna moved to where she could see also. Her eyes grew wide with dismay.

A huge blood-red bruise covered the upper portion of Lucius's shoulders, with a deep laceration across the top. His eyes met Anna's.

"It's all right. It's not your fault."

How had he known what she was thinking? If not for her… She left the thought hanging, refusing to dwell on the possibilities.

"Anna, bring me that bottle of salt," Leah commanded, and Anna hastened across the bedroom, retrieving the vial from the dresser.

"I am fine," Lucius told his mother, starting to rise. She pushed him none too gently back down with her one good arm.

"You have a laceration, Lucius. It needs to be treated before it becomes infected."

Anna started to hand the vial to Leah, but she motioned for Anna to apply it. "You'll have to do it, Anna."

Anna reluctantly moved forward, knowing that with Leah's one paralyzed arm it would be difficult for her to administer the salt. The look in Lucius's eyes set her to trembling. Anna took courage from the fact that Leah seemed to notice nothing amiss.

Leah held down the collar of Lucius's tunic with her good hand while Anna gently applied the salt to the partially open wound on his shoulder. Lucius sucked in a breath between his teeth, his body tensing as the salt burned for several long seconds. Anna could almost feel his pain.

"Now, the aloe," Leah told her.

Anna picked up the vial of aloe mixed with myrrh. Pulling the stopper from the amphora, the scent quickly permeated the room. Pouring some into the palm of her hand, Anna then began carefully working it across the wound on Lucius's shoulder. His muscles relaxed under her ministering touch as the balm soothed the stinging.

The look he gave Anna nearly buckled her knees.

Jumping to his feet, he told them in a voice that brooked no argument, "That's enough. I have to go."

He quickly left the room, but it was some time before Anna was able to breathe properly.

Lucius strode from his mother's room trying to bring his thoughts and feelings back into subjection.

He had gone with the express purpose of finding Anna and trying to discover if her feelings for him were anything like what he felt for her, but he had gotten sidetracked by his mother's wan appearance.

His mind whirled in confusion, his thoughts a jumbled

mixture of what his mother had said and what Anna had been doing.

What had his mother meant when she said that she was a stumbling block to him? How was that even possible? If not for her, he didn't know where he might be. It was only his mother's calming influence that kept him from turning into the monster he sometimes felt himself to be.

And what of Anna? She had grown from an obscure little nothing in his mind to the one thing he could not get out of his thoughts.

Andronicus was waiting for him in the atrium deep in conversation with Petronius. Both their looks swung his way as he approached, and Petronius rose to his feet.

"Your mother? Is she well?"

Was she well? No, doubtless she was not. Was she as stubborn as ever? Definitely.

"She is as well as can be expected."

Petronius pulled a scroll from his toga sleeve and handed it to Lucius. "The name and address of one of Rome's finest physicians is in this. If he can't help your mother, no one can."

Lucius smiled in appreciation. He took the scroll, tapping it against his palm. "I appreciate this more than you can know."

Petronius nodded. "I will leave you now. I believe Andronicus has made the final arrangements for your trip to Rome."

Petronius disappeared into the peristyle and Lucius turned to Andronicus.

"So, everything is ready?"

Andronicus jerked his head in affirmation. "Aye, Tribune. We sail in two days."

Lucius seated himself on one of the couches in the

atrium, leaning back and blowing out a breath. "It can't be too soon for me."

Andronicus smiled. "It will be good to get back to Rome. It will be nice not to have to look over my shoulder everywhere I go, expecting an attack at any minute."

Lucius nodded absently, his attention suddenly arrested by his mother and Anna heading into the triclinium for the evening meal. He could still feel the spot where Anna's cool hand had applied the unguent to his back. His reaction to her surprised him. It had been a long time since he had even noticed a woman, much less desired one.

"You have had some of the most beautiful women in Rome fairly panting after you," Andronicus told him, "and yet you seem to have fixated your attention upon this one little Jewish girl with no looks to speak of."

Lucius glared at him, ready to argue the point, but something in Andronicus's look made him hesitate.

"Are you talking about me, my friend, or yourself? I notice whenever Tapat is about you seem to be preoccupied."

Andronicus's face colored, but he met Lucius's eyes squarely. "What is it about these Jewish women? It's as if once smitten men can never be free of them."

Lucius studied his friend curiously. "Do you want to be?"

Andronicus didn't answer. Shrugging his shoulders, he followed Lucius as he rose to go into the triclinium.

Reclining couches were laid out in a circular pattern around a small table in the center. The frescoes on the walls here were much like his mother's house in Jerusalem, giving the impression of being in Rome.

Lucius chose the couch next to his mother as the two on each side of Anna had already been confiscated by Petronius's daughter and eldest son. Anna was laughing at something they said, her musical voice bringing a smile to more than one face in the vicinity.

Throughout the meal, Lucius found his attention drifting more and more often to Anna. He couldn't seem to help himself, though he noticed that she deliberately ignored him, answering any questions he put to her as briefly as possible. He wasn't certain whether to be vexed or amused.

What were her feelings for him? He knew without conceit that she was attracted to him, he had had enough experience with women to know that, but how deep did those feelings run? He had to know. With that intent, he followed her into the peristyle after the meal was finished and the others had retired for the night.

The moon was a golden orb in the night, reminding him of the night he had found her. She was unaware of his presence and he stood silently watching her for a few minutes. She lifted her face to the night sky, and a beam of reflected moonlight shone fully on her face, giving it an ethereal glow.

He began to wonder if Andronicus might have been right about the attractions of Jewish women, for he found Anna to be more lovely each time he saw her.

He moved forward and she started, turning at his approach. Her eyes went wide and she looked as though she were about to flee in panic.

"The night is beautiful," he told her, trying to put her at ease. He noticed her breathing coming in short bursts. She was truly afraid of him, but she stood quietly as he drew closer. She refused to look him in the eye, instead watching the fish in the fountain. She sat down beside the pool and allowed her fingers to slide through the water.

"It is a beautiful night," she finally answered.

He noticed that much as he had done earlier, she was

fighting to get her emotions under control. He sat on the edge of the fountain and looked into her face.

"Anna, why are you so afraid of me?"

Anna took several deep breaths trying to answer that question herself. He had never been anything but kind to her, so why did she fear him? True, he was a symbol of Roman power and authority, but he had never used that against her.

And then she realized that it wasn't him that she was afraid of, but herself.

"I am not afraid of you, Tribune."

"I thought we had agreed that you would call me Lucius."

She did meet his eyes then, a slight smile quirking her lips. "I'm sorry, but it's hard to see you as anything else when you are always in uniform."

He returned her smile. "Is that what it would take to make you stop looking at me as though I were a lion?"

Anna frowned in bewilderment. What exactly did she want from him? When he was near, some sense of self-preservation made her want to flee from his presence, but when he was gone, she couldn't wait for his return.

"You confuse me, Lucius."

He rose to his feet and his face was cast in shadow when he looked down at her. "Then we are walking the same path, little Anna, because you confuse me, as well."

He lifted a hand to her face, stroking her cheek with his thumb. Surprised by his answer, she forgot to step away. But then, she didn't really want to. His stroking thumb was mesmerizing. Her mind was trying to warn her but she hushed it into silence. This moment had been coming for a long time and was as impossible to revoke as it was for the moon to stop shining.

He bent his head to her, his lips pressing softly against hers until he felt her innocent response. Then he deepened the kiss until Anna thought she would surely faint from the feelings rushing through her. If there had been any doubts before, he had laid them to rest with his kiss. She loved him, more than she realized it was possible to love someone.

But why was he attracted to her? Was she just the closest woman at hand for him to play with and then discard? Having been rejected all of her life, she doubted that a man as handsome and virile as Lucius could truly be attracted to someone like her. That thought broke over her like the cold snow in winter, and she pulled her lips away and tried to move out of his grasp, but he wouldn't release her.

He frowned. "What's wrong?"

"I need to go inside. It's late. Your mother might need me."

Smiling, he tried to pull her back into his arms. "I need you."

She fought him, struggling against his superior grip. He quickly released her, his look one of uncertainty.

"You really are afraid of me, aren't you?"

She didn't know how to answer him. Yes, she was afraid of him, afraid that he would tempt her to forget herself and her vows to her Lord, afraid that when he tired of playing with her he would abandon her for someone more beautiful, more enticing.

But she was more afraid of herself. She was afraid that her faith wasn't strong enough to ward off the seduction of a normal life with a man. A life she could never have with Lucius because he was an unbeliever, and she was very afraid he would never be able to overcome his hatred for his father enough to see past his pain to the only Father that really mattered. As she had done. *Oh, Lord, how could I forget You so quickly? Forgive me.*

"Yes, Lucius, I am afraid of you. You could hurt me in more ways than you can possibly know."

"I would never hurt you," he told her in frustration.

She pushed away the hand he was reaching out to her, and in the moonlight she saw his countenance darken with anger at her rejection.

"Anna…"

Before they could say another thing, Andronicus came into the garden. He glanced from one to the other, one dark brow winging upward.

"The ship's captain is here to see you," he told Lucius. "He has changed his schedule and wishes to leave tomorrow."

"What?"

Lucius glanced at Anna and she could see the struggle he was going through as he tried to determine his priorities. She made the decision for him.

"I have to go."

She could feel him watching her as she left the garden, her heart shattering into a thousand pieces.

Chapter 11

Lucius leaned against the bulwark of the ship and stared out over the Great Sea, the one the Romans called the Mare Nostrum. The sun shone brightly on the choppy blue water, but a dark bank of clouds could be seen from behind far in the distance.

The captain had been adamant about leaving, his joints telling him there was bad weather coming. Lucius snorted, shaking his head at the man's foolishness. It was the beginning of the dry season, yet the man based his shipping on his aching joints.

Andronicus joined him, leaning his forearms against the bulwark. "We're making good time."

Lucius glanced at him and nodded. "We should reach Rome in less than a week at this rate. We'll need to stop in Sicily to replenish supplies, but that should be no problem."

Andronicus studied the sea, but Lucius could tell that something was on the man's mind. He waited, knowing that Andronicus would speak in his own time after he got his thoughts into whatever kind of order necessary to get the information he was looking for.

"Lucius," he finally started. "Your mother and Tapat have been more than master and servant for many years, yet you said that Tapat had responsibilities in Jerusalem. Surely she would have been better suited to be with your mother than Anna."

Lucius reined in his quickly fired temper at the slight to Anna, realizing that Andronicus was making a valid argument, at least from his point of view. If he told Andronicus what kept Tapat in Jerusalem, he had no doubt the man would honor the secret, yet it was not his secret to divulge.

"Tapat is where she needs to be," he told him and left it at that. He could tell that Andronicus wished to question him further but he wisely refrained. He moved from the rail, giving Lucius one last look before he walked away.

Sighing, Lucius returned to his reflections, which inevitably focused on Anna. He was no better than Andronicus, pining after a woman who seemed to be out of his reach. Anna had made certain that they had no time alone together. Every moment had been spent helping his mother to pack and get ready to sail, and every moment since had been spent in the cabin below.

His thoughts inevitably fixated on that kiss in the moonlit garden. He had kissed her, testing the waters so to speak. There was an attraction between them that was like nothing he had ever encountered before, but was it merely his instinct to conquer that was driving him? Or was it perhaps the fact that she had such an aura of peace about her despite what she had been through, and he had hungered after such peace for a long time. The kind of peace that was not brought about by sword and blood, like the Pax Romana, the Roman Peace forced upon conquered countries.

Her innocent response to his kiss had quickly fired a response in him he hadn't been quite prepared for. He had always gone into a relationship knowing what he wanted and was more than happy to end the association when he received it. With Anna, he was plowing new ground. He realized that she was right in what she had said. He could hurt her, and he didn't want to do that.

Her kiss had been hesitant, seeking something from him, and he knew he couldn't give her what she was looking for. He was a man with blood on his hands and fire in his heart, a scarred man. What she needed was a gentle man, one who would share her faith and bring her the happiness she deserved. He was not that man.

Restless, he wandered around the ship checking on his men and making certain that all their supplies were well protected. He had to keep his mind busy to keep it from straying into forbidden territories. If he didn't get this situation with Anna resolved soon, he was going to go mad. It would be best if he stayed away from the woman altogether. As if that was going to happen on a ship in the middle of the sea, he thought wryly.

Still, he had learned long ago how to hide his feelings. It had been necessary to survive both his father and the atrocities that had been a large part of his life for many years. Tenderness of any kind could get a man killed in the world he lived in.

Now the question was, how did he stay away from the very thing that he wanted more than anything?

Anna had seen very little of Lucius for the duration of the trip across the Great Sea. Even in Sicily he managed to avoid her whenever possible, leaving her more confused than ever. If he thought she was going to take advantage of his slight indiscretion in the garden, he could very well think again. And right now, she had more to worry about than a soldier's attempt at seduction. Leah was growing weaker physically, although her mind was astute enough.

"Leah, I cannot accept your generous offer. You have done enough for me already and, in truth, I owe you more than I could ever hope to repay."

Leah tried to make her take the bag of coins again. "I insist, Anna. What will you do if something happens to me? I wish to make certain that you are well cared for. And don't think I don't know why you agreed to leave Jerusalem and come with me."

Anna took the bag of coins and set it on the desk next to the bed in their cabin. She grasped Leah's hands and gently pulled her down onto the edge of the bed beside her.

"I came because you needed me."

Leah shook her head. "No, you came because you love me, just as I love you. You and Tapat have both been like daughters to me." She gave Anna a shrewd look. "I gave the same amount to Tapat and she didn't reject me."

Anna sighed heavily. "Oh, Leah. I am not rejecting you."

Leah's look grew serious. "Anna, I know I haven't much time left in this life. Let me do this for you. I cannot take my money with me, nor would I even try if I could. The Lord would want me to do this for you or He wouldn't have sent you to me."

Trying to hold back the tears, Anna reluctantly took the bag of coins that contained more wealth than she could have ever hoped to receive in her lifetime. Every day she understood a little better Lucius's desperation not to lose this wonderful woman.

"Thank you," she finally whispered huskily and hugged Leah.

Both women had tears in their eyes when Lucius came

into the room. He looked from one to the other, his eyebrow raised in question.

Leah merely smiled at him while Anna took the pouch of coins and went to put it with her things.

"We will be in Rome soon," he told them. "I thought you would like to come on deck and see."

Anna helped Leah wrap her palla around her while picking up her own shawl and placing it around her head and shoulders.

They followed Lucius from the cabin and up the stairs to the deck. It took a moment for their eyes to adjust to the bright sunlight after the dimness of the cabin.

Lucius led them to the side of the ship that faced the part of Rome that had been built on the Palatine Hill, which could be seen several miles away. The sunlight shimmered off the white limestone and marble buildings in the distance.

As they approached, Anna's eyes grew wide with awe at the spectacular sight. Buildings taller than any she had ever seen stretched for as far as the eye could see. She had been amazed by Caesarea Maritima, but she was truly awed by the eternal city of Rome.

Lucius was grinning down at her. "Impressive, isn't it?"

Leah answered him instead. "That remains to be seen."

Lucius merely shook his head, his smile turning wry.

The closer they got to the city, the greater the stench rising to their nostrils. Leah and Anna both placed their shawls over their noses.

"Where is that smell coming from?" Leah asked.

"Rome has a very modern sanitation system," he told them. "All of the city's waste is piped through lead pipes to the river."

Both Leah and Anna gave him a dubious look. "And it always smells like this?" Anna asked.

Lucius grinned again. "You'll get used to it."

Leah gave him a look that spoke volumes. "I am ready to head back to Jerusalem right now."

Lucius returned her look in equal measure. "Don't worry. Where I live, it is far enough away and upwind of the river most of the time."

The wharf where they docked was alive with activity. Lucius told them to stay put while he went to see if the arrangements for a litter to carry them home had been seen to.

"Can we not just walk?" Leah asked.

Lucius's smile was gentle. "No, Mother. It's much too far."

They watched him cross the deck, stopping next to Andronicus. The two men talked together a moment before Lucius strode down the gangplank and Andronicus began yelling orders to the soldiers.

In a short time Lucius was back.

"Come with me."

Lucius took his mother's arm while Anna followed close behind. Magog brought up the rear, his curious look searching the crowds around them.

When they reached the wharf, a litter awaited them with an old man standing next to it. Lucius introduced him as his property manager, Claudius.

Claudius bowed to them and then drew back the drapes of the litter. Lucius helped his mother into the litter and then turned to Anna.

"You, too. It's a double litter."

Anna studied the immobile faces of the Greek slave bearers, sweat beading their brows, and hesitated. As though he could guess the thoughts running though her mind, Lucius told her, "Don't even think about it. Get in."

Reluctantly she climbed in after his mother, settling herself on the cushions across from her. Leah reached up and dropped the side curtains, not wanting to provide a spectacle for others to gawk at.

Lucius climbed on a horse that a servant was holding for him. He glanced around to make certain everyone was ready and nodded. "Let's go."

Periodically as they bumped along, either Leah or Anna would peek out, fascinated by the activity and sights around them.

At one point Lucius pointed out an elephant being led by a Moorish slave. Both Leah and Anna were fascinated by the huge animal.

Rome was like nothing Anna had ever experienced. Although Jerusalem was a mixture of peoples, the streets of Rome were crowded with fair-haired Germans who Lucius explained were the Imperial Guard who guarded the emperor, Egyptians with their shorn heads, Oriental princes and even wild men from Britannia.

When they passed the Roman Forum, they saw the lines of people awaiting the free grain the government handed out. As in Jerusalem, the people were either very rich or very poor; few lived in between. Anna noticed Leah's look of pity and smiled in commiseration with her.

When they arrived at Lucius's villa, Lucius helped Anna from the litter, his eyes holding hers for several seconds before his mother's cough took his attention.

"Are you all right?"

"Just a little thirsty. It was hot in the carrier."

He took her hand. "Then let's get you inside so Claudius can bring us something to slake our thirst."

Anna stared at the villa in amazement. This house was even larger than the one they had left in Jerusalem.

They stopped in the atrium while Lucius made arrangements with the servants to bring in their supplies.

The entrance room was at least twice the size of the one

in Leah's house, the opening in the roof that let in the sunlight showing off the marble tile floor. Frescoes covered the walls here, unlike the entry at Jerusalem. They gave the impression of entering a large temple, with paintings of statues all along the walls that Anna presumed were Roman gods. It made her skin crawl.

"Let's go outside," Leah suggested, her look intimating that she felt the same. "One of the first things I intend to do if I have to live here is have this room repainted."

They moved outside into the peristyle. A large fountain dominated the center of the garden; a beautifully carved statue of a graceful woman dressed in a toga poured water into the pool below her from an upturned urn.

An upper balcony ran the entire perimeter of the garden with doors leading into upstairs rooms, and below the balcony other doors led to downstairs rooms.

Green grass surrounded the fountain for quite a distance, ending at a marble walkway that circled the entire garden. Between the columns that supported the balcony, bushes sported their flowering beauty. Several trees lent their shade to areas of seating strategically placed to give the best view of the garden.

Leah sighed, a look of peace settling across her features. "I think I know where I will spend most of my time."

They stood together enjoying the tranquillity and beauty that surrounded them.

Lucius joined them. "Well, how do you like it?"

"Have you always lived here?" Anna asked him.

"Ever since I was forced to leave Jerusalem. It was Father's house before it became mine."

The memories reflected on his face were not pleasant ones. Anna grieved for the boy who was so ruthlessly torn from his home and mother and brought to this place that, despite its beauty, would have been cold without a mother's love.

Lucius took his mother's arm. "Come into the triclinium. I have arranged for our evening meal to be served earlier than usual because I wanted our first meal in this house to be together, and I have to leave shortly."

He led the way into the dining room. It, too, was larger than the one in Jerusalem. Lucius's father must have been an extremely wealthy man to be able to afford two such homes.

The floor was white marble, the paintings on the wall giving the impression of being outdoors. Unlike the house in Jerusalem, this triclinium had an open door to the outside that allowed the sunlight and air to flow into the room.

At least twenty serving couches that would hold three people each were scattered about the room. Anna and Leah exchanged glances. Strange how they seemed to be so in tune with each other's thoughts. Obviously Lucius's father liked to entertain.

Lucius had some of the servants move three of the couches closer together. A communal table was placed in their midst.

Anna seated herself next to Leah's right and Lucius seated himself to his mother's left. The couches were arranged in a triangular pattern so that whenever Anna glanced up, she could see Lucius intently watching her. As before, her hands grew clammy and her heart thrummed an irregular tempo that told her she was not as unaffected by him as she had hoped to be. She resigned herself to the fact that it was going to be a very uncomfortable meal.

The servants brought the food. The amount and variety would have fed a family of five for at least a week. Guilt made Anna's appetite diminish so that she picked at her food.

"Is the food not to your liking?" Lucius asked her.

Since she wasn't about to tell him the truth, she settled for a half-truth. "I'm just not very hungry."

His look was dubious but he refrained from comment. He turned to his mother. "And you?"

"Everything is delicious but, like Anna, I am not very hungry. I think I am more tired than hungry."

Lucius concentrated on his own food for several minutes before focusing on his mother. "There's something I've always wanted to ask you."

She nodded her head, giving him permission to continue.

"Why have you never been to Rome? Did Jerusalem mean so much to you that you couldn't leave it even for a short time and come to see us?"

The pain Lucius had refused for so many years now swamped him. Whenever he had asked his father why his mother didn't come to them, his father had always told him to stop whining and act like a man. So why was he asking this now? What good could come of knowing why his mother had abandoned him to his father's less-than-tender mercies?

His mother's face turned white and she looked away. She suddenly looked much older than her years.

"Lucius, it would be better not to speak ill of the dead."

Confused, he asked, "Why would telling me this be speaking ill of the dead?"

She got to her feet and Anna rose quickly to stand beside her, obviously noting the color that had leached from his mother's face.

"The past is better left in the past," Leah told him firmly. "We are together now."

Lucius got to his feet, as well. "All those wasted years,

Mother. We could have been there for each other just as we were when I was a child."

She shook her head. "No, we couldn't."

"Why?" His voice truly sounded like the whine his father had accused him of, but he didn't care. He had to know.

"Leave it, Lucius," she demanded, the tears in her eyes telling him there was more to the story than he knew. She started to walk away but he grabbed her arm to keep her in place.

"Tell me!"

At her slight sob, Lucius almost relented but it was something that had eaten away at him all his life. He had to know.

"All right, I'll tell you!" She rounded on him. "He didn't want me anymore!"

The tears were running down her cheeks in a silent river now. It took him several seconds before he fully comprehended what she was trying not to say.

"He was ashamed of you," he almost growled. "That's it, isn't it?"

He suddenly remembered conversations between his father and his Jew-hating friends. Romans considered them atheists because they refused to accept other gods. That and the fact that they were so antisocial. The Greeks had a term for it. *Misanthropia.* Hater of mankind.

Anna placed an arm around his mother's shoulders, her look pleading with him to stop. He ignored her, his emotions raging out of control.

"It was all right to have a Jewish wife when he was in Jerusalem, but not in Rome," he concluded. "After all you gave up, he did that to you?"

His own pain became as nothing in the face of such news. He wished now that he had remained silent. If his father hadn't been dead already, Lucius would have found him and slain him on the spot. His ever-present anger was about to boil over and he needed to leave before he said or did something he might regret.

He pushed past them and quickly headed for the door. "I have to leave. I will be back later." He stopped at the door and glanced back. "Claudius will see to any needs you have."

He slammed the door behind him, his fists clenching and unclenching at his sides. He knew of only one way to release the amount of anger coursing through him. He headed for Mars Field to work out with the legionnaires.

Chapter 12

Anna entered the villa and laid a basket containing fruit on the table near the door. It was the beginning of autumn and the temperatures were still higher than normal. She dropped her shawl next to the fruit, relieved to be free of the stifling garment.

Leah came from the peristyle, her smile warm despite the paleness of her complexion. Lately she had been having more trouble breathing and Anna was worried that something might happen to her before Lucius could return.

He had been sent away shortly after their arrival to some far-flung outpost in the empire, but they knew not where and Anna had no way to get word to him. She had hoped that his leaving would give her the opportunity to bring her fluctuating emotions under control, but it had the opposite effect. She missed him so much it was like a physical ache.

Leah looked over the basket of fruit, frowning at the selection. "This was all you could find?"

Anna nodded, and they both took a seat next to the collecting pool below the roof opening of the atrium. Anna dipped her hand in the pool, patting her throat and face with the cool water.

"The selection has lessened due to the hot weather. They are expecting a new shipment next week."

"Well, we will just have to make do."

Anna noticed the painters working on the far wall. Leah had made good her threat and, with Lucius's permission, was making changes to the villa. Already the place reflected her love of nature. The idol frescoes had been painted over and replaced with a crisscross trellis that extended the entire length of the west wall. Flowering vines appeared to be weaving in and out of the slats. It amazed Anna how realistic the pictures were. Truly the fresco painters were imbued with a talent beyond the ordinary.

The other three walls had been painted to look like the rolling green hills of Rome. She no longer felt like an alien amid a pagan society when she was in this room but, instead, was reminded of Elohim's wonderful creation.

"Will the painters be finished before the Lord's Day?" Anna asked.

"I have been assured that they will."

Anna smiled at Claudius when he brought in a tray with glasses of fruit juice. The mixture of pomegranate and grape was one of her favorites.

"Thank you, Claudius."

He bowed his head and retreated from the room.

Leah turned to her, her eyes sparkling with excitement. "I am thrilled to be hosting the Lord's Day fellowship."

Anna could well understand why. Shortly after arriving in Rome, Leah had made inquiries about the Christian community here. It had surprised and thrilled her to find that Claudius was a believer, and he had led her to a group of believers who were mostly Gentiles but who had welcomed them with open arms. After years of isolation and abuse, Leah had found a new reason to live.

It hadn't taken her long before she was involved with helping the poor here in Rome, which was one of the reasons for having the Lord's Day worship here. It was an opportunity to share what Elohim had blessed her with. It was also one of the reasons for eliminating as quickly as possible the frescoes of the Roman gods.

Claudius returned. "My lady, Tertius would like a word with you about the benevolence baskets."

Leah rose to her feet. "I'll be right there." She smiled at Anna. "Why don't you go into the peristyle? It's too lovely a day to stay inside."

"I agree. I think I will do that."

The garden was Anna's favorite place. Even in the extreme heat, the trees, fountain and bushes made it a cool retreat. It was also a good place to sit and think. Her problem was that her imaginings invariably turned to a handsome Roman with a grudge against her Lord, and she was having difficulty mastering such thoughts. What he needed was a love he was unwilling to accept.

Perhaps a little more prayer time would help.

Lucius stood before the young Emperor Nero and felt the dissatisfaction of a wasted life. How many years had he served men who felt themselves to be gods, only to have them die, sometimes in mysterious ways, and another one take their place?

Nero could have probably been considered handsome by many, but his life of dissipation was beginning to show already at the age of twenty-two. His petulant mouth was turned down as he conferred with his advisers.

Nero finally turned to him. "Tribune Lucius, come forth."

Lucius saluted him with a fist against his chest and then handed him the sealed scroll in his hand.

"You say this is from General Galba?"

"Aye, Majesty."

Lucius didn't miss the look of irritation that crossed the emperor's face. "Very well. I will read this in private. Have you any other news?"

"No, Majesty, but I have a request."

Surprised, Nero studied Lucius a moment before nodding his head for him to continue.

"I would like to be relieved of duty."

Nero's brows lifted upward. "You are one of my most loyal soldiers and one of Rome's most trusted commanders. Why would you ask this now at such a critical time?"

"Majesty, my mother is dying."

Nero glanced at his own mother, Agrippina, who was standing across the room. The look he gave her made Lucius's blood run cold.

"Lucky you," he murmured under his breath, and Lucius felt his skin crawl at the threat he saw in the emperor's eyes. Lucius wouldn't give a silver denarius for the chances of the so-called Augusta. As for himself, he was tired of court intrigue, plots and assassinations. Rome was dying and the stench had reached far out into the empire, bringing the vultures home to roost. There was an essence about the city that was hard to define, a seemingly smoldering evil just waiting to burst into a conflagration.

Lucius tried again. "I have no heirs, Majesty, and a considerable estate to manage."

Nero hesitated. "I hate to let you go."

Lately, Lucius had felt a compulsion to be near his mother, some sense that things weren't right. He didn't know if it was because of her failing health, or because she had claimed this Christian religion and enemies against it were stirring throughout the city. Whatever it was, he didn't want to have to leave her again. He offered up a prayer to his mother's God. *If You are there, I need You now. Please. I need to be with my mother. I need to make up for the years I spent resenting her. I know I have no right to ask this of You but, for her sake, I'm begging.*

"Is there someone you would like to recommend to take your place?"

Lucius wasn't certain whether suggesting someone to his position would be a good thing or a bad.

"I would recommend Centurion Andronicus Lepidus."

Nodding, Nero smiled. "Yes, Andronicus would be a good choice. Very well. You are relieved."

"Thank you, sire."

"And Lucius?"

"Yes, Majesty?"

"Your father had a lot of influence in the empire. I expect the same from you. I would like to see you represent me in the senate."

Lucius hesitated but a second. Having access to the senate would help him keep his finger on the pulse of Rome, which in turn would help him to know best how to protect his mother and Anna. It was the first time he had allowed himself to think of Anna in correlation with his mother. The two had become firmly fixed in his mind as his family, and he would do anything to protect them.

"As you wish, sire."

Saluting again, Lucius hurriedly took his leave before the fickle emperor could change his mind. As tribune, his military accoutrements had been made specifically for him and thereby normally, unlike other legionnaires, his to keep. Since he had no desire to do so, he would pass his outfits along to Andronicus, minus his gladius and sword. He only hoped Andronicus would be pleased with his promotion.

Only one thought was uppermost in his mind right now. He had prayed to his mother's God, and He had answered. Was it just a coincidence?

Another thought followed quickly on its heels. Would Anna now finally see him as a man and not an avenging warrior of Rome?

A sense of someone watching her made Anna glance up. Lucius was standing in the doorway of the peristyle studying her. Her heart leapt in her chest and then settled into that furious rhythm that she had come to associate with being in his presence.

He smiled and she relaxed slightly. It was the first time she had seen him without his military paraphernalia. Even without the fitted chest piece, his blood-red tunic fit tautly across his broad chest and shoulders.

"What are you doing?" he asked.

Smiling, she motioned around at the garden. "I was just helping to remove any weeds that have dared to show themselves in this beautiful garden."

He came toward her and her heartbeat began racing again.

"I see my mother has been busy," he told her. "The atrium now no longer looks like I am walking into the Pantheon."

She studied him to see if he was angry, but his expression was more one of curiosity.

"Do you like it?" she asked.

"The murals are exquisite."

Anna agreed. They were painted by a Jew named Joshua whom Leah had found at their first meeting of the Christians they had attended. He had left Jerusalem when the persecution of Christian Jews had become too severe to remain. Leah had been pleased that they were able to help each other.

Lucius came closer, picked a flower from the bush behind her and placed it behind her ear. He allowed his fingers to slide down her cheek, his eyes dark and intense. Anna swallowed hard at his bold look.

"There are servants to tend the garden," he remonstrated.

She stepped away from him and saw his instant frown.

"I know," she agreed, "but it seems a shame to allow such ugliness to mar such a beautiful garden. I feel compelled to remove them."

She grinned, but he didn't reciprocate. Instead, he took the weed that was in her hand, a spindly thing with a small blue flower.

"Even a weed can be beautiful."

The look he gave her made her think that he was somehow referring to her.

He continued. "All of the beauty in this garden and yet this one lone weed stood out from among it. The beauty here you take for granted after a while. The weeds you notice because they are different, set apart."

That was something she had certainly never considered. Perhaps being a weed in the garden of life was not such a bad thing. Still, she couldn't help remembering Leah's broken voice when she told her son that her husband had no longer wanted her. If a woman as beautiful as Leah could be rejected, how much more so someone as lacking in beauty as Anna herself.

Lucius glanced behind her and stopped suddenly. His eyebrows lifted in surprise. "What happened to the fanum?"

Anna felt that Leah should be the one answering such a

question. The small worship sanctuary had been relegated to a mere sitting alcove.

Lucius swept by her, turning and fixing her with a cautious eye. "What have you done with the statue of Jupiter?"

Anna took a deep breath. "Your mother had it removed."

He frowned. "It was the god my father chose as his patron god."

"I believe your mother found it offensive," she told him softly.

He looked from her to the column that had once held the statue but now held a potted fern.

"I see."

Shrugging, Lucius moved to sit on the edge of the pool that was fed by the fountain. "There is something I've been meaning to ask you." His face softened as he studied her. "How have you managed to forget what your father did to you and forgive him?"

Forget? She would never be able to forget the things her father had done to her. She seated herself on the marble bench that Leah had placed inside the small trellis structure that had been used as the fanum.

"I haven't forgotten anything," she disagreed quietly. "The human mind forgets nothing, but forgiveness is also a choice of the mind. I have chosen to forgive my father, just as my heavenly Father has chosen to forgive me."

He plucked a dry bougainvillea leaf from the ground and crunched it with his fingers. "That is something I can't do."

"Lucius." He looked up at the use of his name, as she so rarely used it. "Your father had power over you for so much of your life while he was alive. Don't let him have that same kind of power over you in death."

His eyes darkened with anger. "What are you saying? My father doesn't control my life."

"No," she agreed. "Your anger does. You are so angry

at your father that it spills over onto everything and everyone you touch."

He slowly rose to his feet and she wondered if she had gone too far. Despite being free of his military uniform, he looked to be a very dangerous man.

"If you don't learn to forgive," she continued, "the peace you are searching for will forever be elusive."

"You sound like an oracle," he told her snidely. "Pray, continue. This is most enlightening."

Something she had heard at one of the fellowship meetings made sense to her now. Perfect love casts out fear, and she loved Lucius enough to want to see him happy. That love gave her courage, made her no longer afraid to speak her mind. Without the power of Christ he would never be free of the anger that drove him.

"And now you're angry at me," she said regretfully.

He sighed heavily. He came and sat next to her on the bench, and the small alcove suddenly seemed much smaller than before. Smiling wryly, he told her, "I'm not angry with you. I asked, after all." He scraped his hand back through his dark hair. "I just don't know how to do what you have done. I don't know how to forgive. And now, knowing what I know about my mother and father, it makes me even angrier."

"Your mother forgave your father and was able to move on with her life. Despite her illness, she is happy."

He caught her look. "And you?"

Was she happy? Not entirely. Although with Leah's generosity she would never have to worry about how to take care of herself, she still didn't know what to do about her own future. A part of her wanted so much to believe that her future included the man sitting beside her, but that was wishful thinking. She looked away.

"I am content."

"Which is not the same thing at all," he said drily.

She decided to change the subject. "When do you have to leave again?"

He accepted her change of subject with a lifted brow. "I don't. I asked to be relieved of duty and the emperor has released me."

Surprised, she smiled widely. "Then you will be able to spend more time with your mother!"

"That was my intention," he agreed.

Claudius came into the garden, searching. He spotted them in the arbor and came to them.

"Tribune, there is a woman here to see you."

Frowning, Lucius rose. He glanced down at Anna. "I will talk further with you later."

Claudius watched him leave, a worried frown puckering his brow.

"Something is bothering you, Claudius?" she asked.

"It's the Lady Valeria."

Curious, Anna crossed to the doorway of the peristyle and glanced into the atrium. A woman had her arms wrapped around Lucius's neck, and she was the most beautiful woman Anna had ever seen. Her dark hair was intricately woven and braided with pearls atop her head. Her dark eyes were lined with kohl, her lips painted pomegranate red. The first thing that entered Anna's mind was that she was seeing the Queen Jezebel of the scriptures in living flesh. Ashamed of the thought, she pulled back and headed for the door that led to her bedchamber.

She tried to deny the pain she felt deep inside, but it came upon her in waves. The weeds in a garden might attract attention, but they were callously pulled up and discarded anyway. It was the beauty that everyone wanted to see.

The pain she couldn't stop, but she ruthlessly denied

the tears that were threatening. It was time to stop living in a dreamworld where everything was perfect. Life just didn't happen that way.

She closed the door to the bedroom behind her and stood looking at the apartment's accessories. She had grown used to all the trappings of wealth, forgetting the life of hardship she had left behind.

Curling up on the sleeping couch, she fought to bring her feelings of inadequacy into subjection. She was a child of Elohim, and He had created her perfectly in the image He meant for her to have. To envy others was a sin. It was the same as saying that Elohim had made a mistake, and that was impossible. The scriptures said that Elohim Himself had knit together each person. A calmness settled over her, dislodging feelings that she felt certain came from the evil one.

She needed to let go of her hidden dreams and open her mind and heart to where the Lord was leading her. And right now that seemed to be caring for Leah.

Chapter 13

Lucius took Valeria by the wrists and gently but firmly set her away from him. He had seen Anna standing in the doorway, the hurt on her face plainly visible, and had almost growled with frustration.

Valeria's mouth pursed out into a pout. "This is the reception I receive after coming all this way to welcome you home?"

Lucius wasn't fooled for a moment. "I take it you have heard that the emperor wants me to sit in the senate."

One dark brow lifted in a supercilious arch and she stepped back, sweeping an all-encompassing look over him as though studying her prey. It was an odd thought to have about one of the most beautiful women in Rome. Valeria was a favorite of the emperor and most of the wealthy men in this city. At one time, even he had been pulled into her web of deceit. She had perfected the art of looking innocent and had fooled many a man. There was nothing even remotely innocent about her.

Unlike Anna, who was completely opposite. Anna was like a breath of fresh air after suffering through the scents of the polluted Tiber. Her very touch could send his pulse rate thundering, something Valeria had never been able to do.

"You make it sound as if that's the only reason I came to see you," Valeria rebuked softly.

"Isn't it?"

She pointedly looked around her. "Aren't you going to offer me a seat?"

Lucius sighed inwardly. He and Valeria had parted ways long ago and he had no desire to run with her company again. Palestine had changed him in some subtle way. Or was it Anna? Or maybe even his mother? Or even Elohim?

That thought brought him up short. It occurred to him that the things his mother had taught him had stayed with him through the years and seemed to be returning to him now in an ever-increasing pressure to submit.

He had never thought to get involved with a woman, especially not a Jewess. His father had made it his goal to erase every semblance of his Jewish blood from Lucius's veins. Anna was right. His father could no longer control his life unless he allowed it.

"Lucius?"

Drawn from his reflections, he blinked at Valeria. "What?"

"You haven't heard a word I've said."

It was clear she found this unacceptable behavior. Men usually hung on her every word, hoping for some tidbit of favor.

"I'm sorry. I have a lot on my mind."

Her face cleared of the frown that showed the subtle wrinkles she took so much care to hide.

"Ah, yes. I heard about your mother."

He might have known. There was no way around it. He would have to invite her in until her curiosity was satisfied.

"Please, come into the peristyle and let's catch up on old times."

A soft hand laid across his forearm kept him from moving forward. "Actually, I came to invite you to go with me to the Marcellus theater. They are showing a few Greek pantomimes and I thought it would be entertaining."

Lucius wrinkled his nose. The stories told through music and dancing had never really appealed to him, but before he could decline she continued.

"I know you prefer the performances of histories by people like Ovid and Catallus, but they are so dreary and boring. I thought after spending so much time in Judea you might enjoy some lighter entertainment."

"I appreciate the thought, Valeria, but I am committed for this afternoon."

That was certainly no lie. He had committed to spending as much time with his mother as he could. He hadn't missed the telltale signs that her health was deteriorating. The physician that Petronius had recommended had been unable to help. He had suggested that his mother had a clot of blood in her brain. Lucius didn't even want to know how he had come by that prognosis. More than likely through the vivisection that Levi had so thoroughly denounced.

Since it was illegal to cut on a dead body, many physicians took the bodies of people who hadn't yet passed on and cut them open to study their insides. Usually, gladiators from the arena, but there was also the illegal confiscation of bodies left at the temple of Asclepius or soldiers who had fallen on the field. Lucius shivered. He couldn't decide which was worse, cutting on a live body or a dead one.

Valeria's narrowed eyes told him that she didn't believe him. "Maybe another time then."

He wasn't about to commit himself. "Maybe."

A banging at the front door interrupted their standoff. Claudius went to answer it but Lucius stopped him with a raised palm. "I'll get it, Claudius." He looked at Valeria. "You should probably hurry if you are going to make the first performance."

She gave him a frosty smile. "Of course."

They walked to the door together. Lucius opened it to find Andronicus on the other side.

Andronicus looked from one to the other, taking in the situation at a glance. He smiled at Valeria.

"Hello, Valeria. I haven't seen you in some time."

The smile she gave Andronicus was full of warmth. "Hello, Andronicus. Congratulations on your promotion."

Andronicus turned a surprised look on Lucius in question, but Lucius merely shrugged. The heavens alone knew where Valeria got her information.

"Thank you. I didn't mean to interrupt," he told them. "I can come back another time."

Valeria gave Lucius an unfriendly look. "Not at all. It seems our business is finished."

She passed Andronicus, leaving a drifting scent of fragrance in her wake. They watched as she climbed in her litter and disappeared from view.

"Why is it," Andronicus asked, "whenever Valeria leaves a room I feel as though I have just missed being struck by a cobra?"

Lucius grinned. "My thoughts exactly."

Andronicus shook his head. "Anyway, I wanted to come and thank you."

Lucius stood aside to allow him to enter. He didn't pretend not to know what his friend was talking about.

"I wasn't certain whether you would be pleased or not."

"I go away for a short time and come back to find I have been promoted to tribune. What's not to be pleased about?"

Lucius motioned for him to have a seat in the atrium and for Claudius to bring them something to drink.

Andronicus studied Lucius closely, his lips pressing tightly together. Taking a deep breath, he told Lucius, "I will miss you, my friend."

"As I will you."

"It has been an honor to serve with you. I will miss our companionship."

Lucius took the tray Claudius handed him and set it on the cedar table beside him. He thanked Claudius and handed Andronicus one of the silver goblets of wine.

"You know you are welcome here anytime. Please don't make yourself a stranger."

Andronicus took the proffered cup. "I'm being returned to Jerusalem."

Surprised, Lucius frowned. "Why?"

"The unrest there is growing and Nero knows that I have developed a network of spies."

It bothered Lucius that he wouldn't be there to have his friend's back. They two had been a formidable foe wherever they were sent. Andronicus was more like a brother than anything else.

"Take care, my friend."

"Always."

Lucius changed the subject. "Perhaps you will see Tapat."

Andronicus threw him a sly smile. "Perhaps. At least, if I have anything to say about it. I thought perhaps I could take a message to her from your mother."

Stepping beyond the bounds of friendship, Lucius warned him, "Don't hurt her, Andronicus."

Their glances collided, each searching and finding hidden messages.

"It was not my intention. Does your mother know where I can find her?"

Lucius set his goblet aside. "Let's go and find out."

Lucius glanced up from studying his accounts in the bibliotheca to find his mother standing in the doorway. Surprised, he set down his stylus and pushed the pot of inkblack aside.

"Mother? Is something wrong?"

She glided into the room with the grace he always associated with her. Even with her body half paralyzed, she walked like a queen.

She sat down in the chair opposite his desk and gave him a look that portended trouble. Lucius tensed, steeling himself for what she was about to say.

"I have put off talking about your father for too long. It is time we get some things out in the open."

Lucius froze. Of all the subjects he had prepared himself for, this was the last.

"I thought you said it was wrong to speak ill of the dead."

She sighed heavily. "I was wrong to try to protect myself at the expense of your father."

Blinking, Lucius sat silent not knowing what to say. Every muscle in his body went rigid.

"Lucius," his mother began, "it takes two to end a marriage."

He frowned, not certain he liked where this was going. "What is that supposed to mean?"

"I have allowed your father to take all the blame for the breakup of our marriage. I was wrong."

He opened his mouth to speak, but she held up a hand

to silence him. "Please allow me to have my say without interrupting me."

He could already feel the stirrings of anger that were ever present when his father was discussed. Trying to stifle them, he picked up the stylus again and began twirling it through his fingers, focusing on the back-and-forth movement. Taking a deep breath, he told her, "Go ahead."

"There was no formal marriage between your father and me."

Lucius glanced up. "I know that. He was in the army and that's forbidden." It hadn't really bothered Lucius since most of the legionnaires did the same thing. It was a foolish law and the troops had found a way to circumvent it. They either married anyway without anyone knowing it, or they just chose to live together as man and wife.

His mother leaned forward. "To a Roman this means nothing, but to a Jew it is a deadly sin."

He knew that, as well. "But you did it anyway." It was not a question.

She sat back again and sighed. "I was young and in love. I know that's no excuse, but I was headstrong and determined."

Nothing had changed much in the intervening years. She was still as headstrong and determined as ever, even with a failing heart.

"Even when your father was recalled to Rome and we were apart all those years, I never stopped loving him."

The stylus snapped in Lucius's hand. "How could you, Mother? He was a monster."

Leah's face creased in anger. "He was what Rome made him."

Lucius couldn't argue with her there. Hadn't he felt the same way about himself lately?

"By the time he was recalled to Rome we were already

beginning to have problems. I tried to be everything your father wanted me to be. I changed my appearance, the way I dressed, even the foods I ate, but I just couldn't give up my faith in the one true God. Your father hated what he considered my atheistic views. He thought he could change me, and he did. But into something I hated."

Lucius rose and began pacing. "I don't understand. Father has been dead for years, yet you kept to Roman ways. Why?"

He had to strain to hear her whispered voice. "I didn't want you to hate me, too."

He whirled to face her. Closing the distance between them, he fell on his knees before her. "I could never hate you!" he growled in astonishment. "How could you think that?"

"I knew how much you resented me for not coming to Rome."

He couldn't argue with that. Resented yes, but never hated. There were so many things he didn't understand, and he wasn't certain he wanted to. Some things were better left alone.

"Your father told me that the only way he would allow me to come to Rome was if I would renounce my God and embrace the Roman gods. That I just couldn't do, not even for you, Lucius."

Lucius slowly rose to his feet, eyes flashing, nostrils flaring. "Did you really think that I would be like Father? Have I ever asked you to deny your God?"

"He's your God, too, Lucius," she told him quietly.

He didn't bother to deny it. His mother's teachings had remained with him throughout his life despite his father's attempt to strip them away. When faced with death on the battlefield, it wasn't the gods of Rome that he had called to. Afterward he would belittle his own need to call on any deity, but it didn't change the fact that he had.

"But you have become a Christian."

She then explained to him about Jesus and the fulfillment of the scriptures. A man who was supposedly God, but also the Son of God. It made his head ache just to think about it.

"So this Jesus, this god-man, was meant to die so that everyone's sins might be forgiven."

She got up and came to stand in front of him, her look compelling. "Everyone who will come to Him and accept his Lordship."

"And how can you expect me to change the feelings I have about Father after what you have just told me? How can you expect me to just forgive and forget?"

He pushed away from her and began pacing the room again. He shoved an agitated hand through his hair, glancing her way.

"Son, there are things you need to know about your father, about his past. Things that made him into the man that he was."

Lucius could see that she was tiring and that the strain of this conversation was wearing on her. He gently forced her back into the chair she had deserted and knelt again at her feet.

"It doesn't matter," he told her softly. "It's in the past."

She grabbed his hand. "But it's not! If you believed that, you would be able to forgive him and move on with your life. Don't think that I don't know why you have never settled down with a woman."

His mouth parted in surprise. Now what was on her mind? "You know I could not marry as long as I was in the army."

"No!" she protested. "You are afraid. You are afraid that you will be like him."

His hands clenched into fists, and sparks of self-hatred shot from his eyes. "I am like him!"

She leaned forward in entreaty. "No! You are nothing like him!"

His look turned outward. "Everywhere I went, I was reminded what a fine officer he was, and everywhere I went I was told how much like him I was. Even my battle strategies were compared to his."

Leah placed her good hand against his cheek and turned him to face her. "Yes, you are a fine leader. So was your father. But being a good leader doesn't necessarily make you a good father."

His eyes meshed with hers. "Or a good husband?"

She smiled sadly. "Or a good husband."

Lucius sat on the floor, tucking his feet beneath him. He took her hand into his. "Tell me then what it is you want to tell me about Father that you think excuses him for the man he was."

She squeezed his hand slightly in understanding. "There are no excuses, but there are conditions that mold us into the people that we are. Your father's parents died when he was young and he was sent to live with an uncle and aunt. They were not kind people. He was often beaten, and sometimes starved when he disobeyed. He had to be tough to survive."

"I never knew that."

She shook her head. "No, he rarely mentioned it, but it colored his thinking. He was afraid that something like that might happen to you if he was killed. It's why he sent you away to Rome. That and the fact that he wanted you away from my influence of our Jewish God."

She looked down at him then. "Can you deny that your

father is the reason you grew into the strong man that you are?"

He sighed. Like his father, he had learned to be tough to survive. "No, I guess not, but that still doesn't excuse him. What of kindness? What of love?"

"You had a mother to give you that. He had no one. The Roman army is not the place to learn about love. He loved you as much as it was possible for him to love anyone."

Lucius smiled wryly. He could feel the thin texture of her skin against his rough fingers and knew that his time with his mother was going to be very short. His chest became so tight he could hardly breathe. She wanted so much for him to let go of the past and, if there were any way possible, he would do that just to make her happy. But he still didn't know how.

"Do you really believe that?"

"I know it. Why do you think he used his influence and wealth to procure you an officership? He was so proud of you, of what you became."

"And what of you?"

How could his father have stopped loving his mother? How could anyone? She was the most lovable and kind person he had ever known. She was always helping those in need, always giving and never asking for anything in return.

"I forgave your father when I accepted Christ as my savior. Just as He forgave me, I in turn extended that forgiveness to everyone who had ever wronged me."

Lucius lifted a brow. "Including your father."

She smiled. "Yes. But I was the one who needed to ask forgiveness of him. I am the one who disobeyed him, who turned my back on my faith."

"Is your illness then His repayment for you leaving your faith?"

She frowned at him, clenching his hand as tightly as it was possible for her to do so in her weakened state. "No! Never! I have told you, Lucius, we all have to die. It is my time. Things have been set right and are being set right. My purpose here on Elohim's earth has been concluded."

"And what about me? What will I become without you?"

She got up from the chair and smiled down at him. "You will become the man of God I know you can be. I've given you much to think about. I will leave you alone now and retire to my bedroom. I'm suddenly very tired."

He started to rise but she laid a hand on his shoulder. "I can manage on my own." Her look became mischievous. "I believe Anna is in the peristyle. The fresh air will do you good."

She left him sitting there, his mind whirling with confused thoughts.

Chapter 14

Anna surreptitiously watched Lucius from across the room as he sat talking with his mother after the group that gathered here each Lord's Day had finished with the communal meal. Many people called it a love feast, but it was not the kind of love that they supposed. The pagan Romans were used to a very different kind of love feast, a feast of sensuousness. For Christians, it was all about brotherly love, a love that met one another's needs in spiritual ways.

Lucius had been sitting in on their worship services for the last several weeks, more to spend time with Leah than anything else. Still, Anna had hope that the things they discussed, the letters they read from the apostles, the faith of this mixture of people, would eventually reach past the pain in his heart and free him of what she had come to discover was his own self-loathing.

He glanced up and caught her watching him. Leah's look followed his and she smiled at Anna. She said something to Lucius and he kissed her cheek and rose to his feet. He was coming across the room and Anna's heart accelerated to such a rate that she could feel her body tingling with expectation.

Lucius took the seat beside her, cocking his head as he studied her. She could feel the heat burning in her cheeks. What exactly did he see when he looked at her? Unlike Valeria, she used no artifices except an occasional elaborate hairstyle that her maid Timna liked to experiment with. Today she was her normal self. Dark hair, dark eyes, dark skin. Nothing like the Lady Valeria.

"You seemed deep in thought," Lucius told her.

She smiled. "Not so deep. My mind was circling in too many different directions to be in deep thought."

"Did any of those thoughts have to do with me?" he asked, his throaty voice causing little butterflies to wing their way around her stomach.

She focused on her hands twining nervously in her lap. No matter how many times she rebuked herself, she just couldn't stop the effect he had on her. The kiss they had shared was forged permanently into her mind.

"In fact, they were," she answered softly. "I was thinking how happy you have made your mother and how content she has become even away from her beloved Judea."

Lucius frowned, glancing back at his mother. "I still wonder if I did right by bringing her here."

Anna gently laid a hand on his arm. The warmth of his skin slid up her fingers, warming her more thoroughly than the burning lamps scattered about the room.

Lucius glanced from where her hand rested into her eyes. His searching look told her that he was equally affected by their physical contact. His lips parted slightly and he focused on her lips. She quickly pulled her hand away and turned to study the room, willing her heart to stop its hectic drumbeat.

"Your mother is not sorry that she came. She is happier than I have seen her in some time."

"And you?"

How to answer that? Her confused feelings had her joyful one day and near despair another. There was no way around it. Leah was going to die soon and Anna would lose both her and Lucius. When Leah was gone, there would be no reason for her to stay. The happiness Leah had brought to her life would stay with her forever, but knowing that she was with the Lord brought equal parts joy and pain.

"I have no regrets," she told him.

She could feel him willing her to look at him, but she refused. This was the Lord's Day, a day to focus her thoughts and feelings on Him, not her own selfish desires.

"I understand there is to be a man coming to speak," he mentioned.

The thrill of Lucius's touch paled in comparison to the excitement that raced through her at mention of the man who was coming to speak to their gathering. He was a Roman who had seen the Lord Jesus when he walked the earth in Palestine. How could she have forgotten such an important guest? It was just another indication that Lucius had such a hold over her thoughts and feelings that she could think of little else when he was around, and even when he was not.

She turned to him, brown eyes glittering with anticipation. "I don't know much about him, only that he was alive and in Palestine when Jesus walked the earth."

He started to answer her, but a commotion at the door turned their attention that way. The room came alive with excited chatter, everyone straining to see the man who had entered.

His bearing when he walked into the room gave credence to the fact that this man had once been an officer in Rome's army. He surveyed the room much like a general inspecting his troops.

Anna saw Lucius rise to his feet, his eyes wide in surprise. She glanced from him to the other man and saw equal recognition and surprise.

"General Atticus!"

Lucius stood frozen to the spot. This was their guest speaker? This was the man of God who had seen Jesus? How was this possible? General Atticus had been one of Rome's finest generals before he retired. Unlike many, he was honest and trustworthy and his men would follow him anywhere, even into death. Much as those under Lucius's command had felt about him.

The general crossed to stand before Lucius.

"Lucius Tindarium! Whatever are you doing here?"

Lucius shook himself from his shocked stupor. "This is my home."

Bushy eyebrows lifted in surprise, the general gave him a searching look. "You are a follower of the Christ?"

The question unnerved Lucius. Was this a trap set by Rome to seek out and find those who would refuse to worship the emperor? Thoughts zinged through his mind as he tried to overcome the shock enough to think things through to protect his mother.

His mother joined them before Lucius could think of a reply. She held out her hand to the general.

"Welcome to my home," she told him graciously, and the general glared at Lucius suspiciously.

"This is my mother," he told him and saw the other man relax slightly.

General Atticus took Leah's hand and raised it to his

lips. "I am pleased to meet you, dear lady. I have heard much about you and the good you are doing in this city."

The surprises just kept coming. What was the general talking about? What good was his mother doing?

"Thank you, General."

The general smiled in return. "Please, call me Atticus. I haven't been a general for many years."

Leah looked from Lucius to Anna. "Allow me to introduce my best helper. This is Anna. She is from Bethany in Judea, and I hope one day to call her my daughter-in-law."

Lucius saw Anna's face turn the color of a ripe pomegranate. Evidently she could no more think of anything to say to such a bold statement than he could.

"I am pleased to meet you," the general said, before turning back to Leah. "I am sorry I was so late, but something came up that I had to attend to."

Leah took his arm and they walked away, his mother's voice floating over her shoulder. "That is quite all right. We weren't certain that you would be able to make it today anyway."

Lucius slowly lowered himself to the reclining couch next to Anna. He glanced over at her and his lips twitched as she looked everywhere but at him.

The idea of Anna as his wife held great appeal for him, but did she feel the same way? Before he could ask, his mother rang a bell to silence the room. She introduced the general and then sat down and gave the floor to him.

Atticus looked about the room, gauging each person's interest.

"Many years ago I was stationed in Jerusalem. A man was brought to trial for being an insurrectionist. This man's name was Jesus." He had to wait for the murmurs to quiet before he could continue.

"I was one of the soldiers who nailed Jesus to the cross."

Shock waves rippled throughout the room. Some voices grew angry, but the general hushed the crowd again with a raised hand.

"I was one of the men who sat at Jesus's feet gambling for His clothing. I am also the one who pierced his side with a spear."

Lucius watched the general, unable to believe what he was hearing.

"I saw so many things that day that could only have come from God. The sky darkened for three hours. The ground shook as I had never felt it shake before. The violence of it caused rocks to break apart."

Lucius frowned. Could this possibly be true? He glanced at Anna and saw that she was mesmerized by the speaker. He had never seen her look so excited, even at the chariot races.

The general continued. "I heard Jesus forgive a thief who had previously cursed Him. I heard Him ask forgiveness for me, as well. The only thought that entered my head that day after seeing everything I saw was that Jesus was surely a God. I searched out the apostles later. I had a hard time finding them as they had gone underground, but I finally located the Apostle Peter."

Someone handed the general a drink and he thanked him, wetting his throat before he continued.

"I am thankful that God is a God of forgiveness. He forgave Peter for betraying Him and Peter helped me to see that He forgave me, as well. From that moment on, my life was changed. Peter baptized me in the Jordan River, and I have tried to follow my Lord ever since."

So many people started yelling out questions that it was hard to differentiate any particular one. The general held up his hand and the room quieted.

"I will be glad to answer any questions you have but, please, one at a time."

The questions came more orderly after that. Lucius heard very little of what they said, his mind trying to work its way around the fact that General Atticus had been a Christian for many years.

It was many hours later before the general took his leave. Lucius watched him go, a host of questions churning in his mind.

Anna settled on the edge of the fountain in the peristyle. She glanced up at the statue of the woman pouring the water from a jug into the basin below and marveled at how realistic the statue was.

"She is one of the Danaides."

Lucius's voice coming from the dark made her jump. Placing a hand on her breast where her heart was dancing and gyrating, she gave him a withering look. "You surely frightened ten years from my life."

He merely grinned, and Anna turned back to inspecting the fountain to keep from looking at him.

"Who are the Danaides?"

He came and sat down next to her, and she felt his presence with every fiber of her being. He pushed her hair back behind her shoulder in a familiar gesture, allowing his hand to rest on her shoulder. Her heart, which had calmed after her fright, now took new wings. When she refused to face him, he let his hand slide off her shoulder.

"The Danaides were daughters of Danaus. They killed their husbands on their wedding night and were condemned in Hades to pour water incessantly into a bottomless well."

Anna stared at him in horror. She glanced up at the statue, no longer seeing its beauty.

Lucius smirked. "Perhaps I should not have told you that."

She lifted a skeptical brow. "Are you jesting with me?"

His eyes danced with humor. "No. It was a favorite story of my father's, hence the statue. Don't ask me why, because I couldn't tell you."

Anna lowered her voice. "Does your mother know?"

"I doubt it, and I would appreciate it if you didn't make it known to her. There's no telling what she would do with the fountain."

That was certainly true. Leah had been ruthless in eradicating any appearance of Roman gods and superstitions.

They both dropped into silence, but it was a comfortable one. At least until Lucius decided to bring up the subject of his mother's pronouncement to the general.

"Anna, about what my mother said this morning."

She jumped to her feet, her face coloring hotly. "Please. Let's not talk about it. I am sorry you were embarrassed but, truly, I have said nothing to make her think such a thing."

He rose to stand beside her and caught her by the arm when she would have walked away.

"I wasn't embarrassed at all. It was something I have been thinking on myself."

She stared up at him in wonder. "Truly?"

He nodded, stroking her face with the back of his hand. "I have known for some time that it would please my mother greatly to see us married."

Anna's face cleared of all emotion as she struggled to get her feelings under control. She should have known. Lucius would do anything to make his mother happy in her last days, and it was obvious that she thought Lucius and Anna would make a good couple.

Pulling away from his touch, she moved away from him

to the grassy part of the garden. She bent and picked up a rock that had become misplaced from the border, setting it back into its place.

"Anna?"

"Was I to be consulted in this plan?"

His brows knit in confusion. "Do you object?"

"Are you surprised? Was I supposed to fall at your feet with gratitude?"

His look of astonishment was equal to her own feelings. Why was she acting this way? It was so out of character for her to be so hateful, especially when she wanted more than anything the very thing he was suggesting. Perhaps after years of having it done to her, she was a little tired of being taken for granted as though she had no intellect of her own.

His face flushed with anger. "I apologize. I had no idea the thought would be so distasteful to you."

All ire fled. "It would not," she told him contritely. "It's just something I can't consider right now."

He came close again, but she couldn't read his face because there were no lamps in this part of the garden.

"Could you if you loved me?"

She opened her mouth to tell him that she already did but snapped it shut just in time. She tried to move away from him again, but he wouldn't allow it.

"No, don't run away. Talk to me."

He grasped her upper arms and pulled her close, his searching eyes pinning her in place as effectively as a spear.

"I think you feel the same way I do, Anna. Do you? Do you love me?"

Her mouth parted in surprise. What was he saying? Was he truly telling her that he loved her?

"You love me?"

Smiling wryly, his hold gentled and he slid his hands up to cup her face. "What did you think I was trying to say?"

Anna was too stunned to think coherently. "But...how? Why?"

"I think I've known from the first moment I saw you lying there in the desert that our lives were somehow entwined."

"But what about Valeria?"

How was it possible that he could care for her over such a beautiful woman? Or did he really? Was he perhaps just trying to win her over to make his mother happy?

"Valeria is nothing to me and hasn't been for a very long time. I have never felt for a woman what I feel for you. I want you to marry me."

Anna's burning joy quickly turned to ashes. As much as she loved Lucius, as much as she loved Leah, she couldn't agree to such a marriage.

She shook her head regretfully. "I can't marry you, Lucius."

He slowly dropped his hands to his side. "Because I'm not a Jew?"

"No. Because you are not a Christian."

He reached for her again, but she stepped out of his way. His hands curled into fists at his sides.

"I don't care if you are a Christian. My mother is a Christian. You can worship whatever God you want to. I won't try to stop you."

How could she make him understand? "When I marry, *if* I marry, I want to share the most important thing in my life with my husband, and that thing is the Lord."

She wondered at his darkening countenance until he stepped forward and wrapped her in a secure embrace.

"Can you truly say that you could allow another man to hold you like this when you know your heart belongs to me?"

No, she couldn't, but since no other man had shown such

interest in her, she doubted she would have to put it to the test. Wherever she went, she knew that her heart would be forever tied to this man. Still, she knew that she would no longer fear a future of being alone. Jesus had forbidden her to be yoked together with an unbeliever, and the apostle Paul had said that it was better to remain unmarried and devote oneself to the Lord. Although she would forever feel like a part of her was missing, she knew that she could face the future with Christ by her side.

"You can't say so, can you?"

Wordlessly, she shook her head.

"Anna," he whispered before closing his lips over hers. The feelings he aroused in her were exquisite torture. He was offering her the very thing she had longed for all her life, but without Christ, those things were meaningless. Ashes in the wind. Coming back to reality, she struggled against his hold, pulling her lips from his.

Reluctantly, he let her go. "You're turning me down?"

She could hear the pain in his voice and she almost relented, but better a little pain now than a lifetime of regret. She had no desire for history to repeat itself and find herself in the same situation as Leah and her husband.

She ached to place her palm against his cheek, to give him comfort, but the only comfort she could give him was the love of God.

"It's not that I don't love you, Lucius. It's just that I love the Lord more."

He stood like an immovable statue for several seconds before he turned on his heels and walked away.

Chapter 15

Lucius stood looking up at the insulae, wondering how one of Rome's greatest generals had been reduced to living in such a ratty apartment.

It had taken him two days to locate the general. No one in the army had known where he had disappeared to, and the Christians had been strangely reluctant to give him the information. It was only because of his mother that he found himself here now.

He was only just beginning to understand how entrenched his mother had become in this Christian cult, yet he couldn't totally refute the religion until he had talked to Atticus. Had the man's time in Jerusalem left him devoid of his senses? But if that were so, how could he have continued to command troops so decisively?

Climbing the stairs in the dark hallway to the apartment above, he hesitated just outside the door. Why was he even here? If he were honest with himself, he would admit that it was because of Anna's rejection. What would make a lonely young woman reject a lover's suit in favor of an invisible God?

In fact, what would make a mother choose this God over her only son?

Women were emotional beings, easily swayed by promises of eternal love, but what about the general? It had to be because of this religion that Atticus had been reduced to penury. Rome favored her retired troops with an allowance and, for generals who had excelled, it was a significant amount. So what was the general's story? To understand Anna's rejection of his suit, he had to find out.

He firmly rapped on the portal, hoping that the general would be home and able to answer some of his questions.

He heard movement within and the door opened slightly and a woman peered out. She looked to be about the same age as his mother, but whereas his mother's appearance was usually perfectly manicured, this woman was ragged. Her gray hair hung long down her back, her face devoid of any semblance of makeup, yet her eyes glowed with an inner light that made her look almost beautiful.

"May I help you?"

Lucius pulled himself together. "I am looking for General Atticus."

She looked him up and down. "And you are?"

"My name is Lucius Tindarium. I served under the general at one time." He tried to see past her into the room. "I hoped to catch up on old times with him."

Lucius heard a voice from inside the apartment. "Let him in, Abigail."

Abigail moved to the side, still studying Lucius curiously. He eased past her, searching the room until he found Atticus seated at a desk. He put down the stylus he was holding.

"Come in, Lucius. It's good to see you again. Allow me to introduce my wife, Abigail."

Lucius dipped his head slightly. "Pleased to meet you."

She smiled. "And you."

Atticus glanced past Lucius. "Didn't you have some things to get at the market, my dear?"

Abigail glanced from Lucius back to Atticus. "I do at that. I will go and see if Livia would like to go with me."

Atticus nodded, then turned his look back to Lucius. "Pull up a stool and have a seat."

Lucius peered around the dark apartment before he finally spotted two stools in the corner of the room next to a small table. Even in the dimness of the apartment he could see the plaster chipping from the walls. A door led to another room, which he supposed was the place where they slept. Most apartments had only two rooms, sometimes only one. Thinking of his own spacious home, he frowned. He wanted to ask about the general's reduced circumstances but knew it wasn't his place to do so.

Lucius set the stool in front of the desk and seated himself, his size and weight making the stool creak alarmingly.

Atticus leaned back in his chair. "What can I do for you, Lucius? Had you wanted to talk over old times we could have done so at your house."

Leaning forward, Lucius fixed him with a compelling look. "Is what you said at the meeting true?"

Atticus gave a wry smile. "I thought that might be what brought you here. Yes. Yes, it's all true."

Lucius studied him, carefully searching for some sign of lunacy, but the bright eyes that met his were clear and lucid.

"You really believe this man Jesus was some kind of demigod and yet He allowed Himself to be crucified?"

Atticus shook his head. "Not a demigod, no, but the Son of God. And yet, more than that. Actually God in the flesh."

How was that even possible? Emperors believed themselves to be gods; had this Jesus believed such a thing about Himself? "I don't understand."

"I'm not surprised. I've been a Christian for many years, yet I still don't understand. It's what we call faith."

Lucius settled more firmly on the stool. "Tell me."

Atticus began with the Jewish scriptures, many Lucius was familiar with. So many prophecies predicted the time of Jesus's birth, life and death. He had learned most of them when he was a child and his mother would tell him stories before putting him to bed. When Atticus came to the part about the crucifixion, Lucius interrupted.

"You say He allowed Himself to die as a sacrifice so that mankind could be forgiven of their sins. You mean Jews, don't you?"

Atticus smiled, shaking his head. He leaned back in his seat, steepling his fingers together. "No, I mean everyone. Even you."

Lucius glanced around the apartment. "Is this what this faith in a Jewish God has gotten you? A life of destitution?"

"No, this is what my refusal to worship the emperor has gotten me. Nero would like to see me dead, but he fears the troops if something should happen to me."

Lucius thought it an appropriate fear. The men loved and revered Atticus, much as they did General Galba. It would be better to let him live with a life of regrets than to kill him. Yet Lucius could see no sign of regret. In fact, the general seemed more content than Lucius with all his wealth.

"It's the woman, Anna, that has brought you here, isn't it?"

Surprised at his perception, Lucius didn't bother to deny it. "She's not like any woman I have ever known."

A knowing smile curled the general's lips. "And what exactly is it that makes her so different?"

Lucius knew he had to be honest. Regardless of how much he might try to deny it, he had to accept it. "I know that it has to do with her God."

"God is reaching out to you through her," Atticus told him earnestly.

Lucius shook his head slowly, doubtfully, yet he knew in his heart it was true. He had been feeling that pull ever since Anna had come into his life. Things his mother had taught him as a small child had come back to him after so many years of being buried deep in his mind and heart.

The Messiah. Could it be true? He felt a hunger deep in his soul, a hunger that could only be assuaged by knowing the truth.

"Tell me," he pleaded with Atticus. "Tell me everything."

Anna was helping Claudius in the kitchen when Leah's maid came running into the room.

"My lady, hurry! It's the mistress!"

Anna dropped the knife she was using to carve the rack of lamb. Grabbing a towel, she hurried from the room after the maid.

"What is it, Bithia? What's happened?"

"I don't know! I found her on the floor in her bedroom. I can't wake her."

Anna and Claudius quickly followed the maid through the atrium and across the peristyle until they reached the outside door to Leah's bedroom. Leah had chosen this room because it was closest to the fountain, and she found the spewing of the water into the basin from the statue comforting.

Anna didn't bother to knock but pushed open the door and entered the room. She was as familiar with this room as her own, having spent many hours here with Leah.

Claudius slowly followed her into the room, took one look at Leah lying on the floor and rushed to help Anna get her onto the bed.

Anna turned to the maid. "Bithia, find Magog and tell him to find Lucius quickly." She wasn't certain where he had gone, but she knew Magog wouldn't give up until he found him.

"What can I do?" Claudius wanted to know.

Anna shook her head helplessly. "I don't know. Would you mind going for the physician?"

Claudius turned and left without a word.

Anna brushed the hair away from Leah's face, noting that her skin was cold and clammy, her breathing almost nonexistent.

"Leah? Leah, can you hear me?"

There was no response of any kind.

"Dear Father, please don't let her die!" Her prayer was a heartfelt one, forcing her worry to the back of her mind.

Not knowing what else to do, she got a basin and collected some of the cool water from the fountain. She retrieved a cloth from the kitchen and, dipping it in the water, began to wipe it over Leah's face and neck. She set the basin aside and took Leah's hand into hers, rubbing it gently as though she could impart some of her own warmth and vitality. Pulling their clutched hands to her forehead, she pleaded softly, "Please, Lord. Not yet. Lucius needs her." Remembering what Lucius had said about making war on God, her stomach clenched tightly with fear for him.

She heard the front door open and hurried through the peristyle into the atrium. Lucius stood inside the doorway, dropping his cape onto the cabinet by the door. He glanced up and saw Anna standing there. A smile lit his face and she realized that he couldn't possibly know what had happened.

"Just the person I was looking for," he told her, grinning. "I have something to tell you."

He crossed quickly to her side but, seeing the look on her face, stopped just short of her. The smile slowly disappeared from his face. "What is it? What's wrong?"

"It's your mother."

His eyes went wide. "Where?"

"In her room."

He pushed past her and ran out of the atrium, Anna following after him.

When she entered the bedroom, Lucius already had his mother in his arms. His face was devoid of color and he looked at Anna helplessly. "Did you send for the physician?"

Anna nodded, feeling just as helpless.

"What can we do?" he asked, and Anna's heart nearly broke at his look of vulnerability.

She doubted he would like hearing it, but it was all she could think of to do at this point. "We can pray," she suggested, although she had been doing so ever since entering this room.

A look of relief swept across his face. "Yes! Yes, let's do that."

Surprised at his acquiescence, Anna moved closer and took his hand as he bent over his mother's prone figure. Before she could utter a word, Lucius spoke fervently.

"Please, Elohim. Don't take her from me just yet. I've only come to know You recently, and I know that I have no reason to expect You to listen to me now, but I'm begging You to give me more time with my mother." He stopped, choking back sobs. "But if it is Your will that she leave me today, at least give me one last time with her to tell her that I have accepted You and that I love You."

Anna dropped onto the chair behind her, her mouth

parted in shock. How had this come about? When had this come about? Could it be true, or was he only trying to bring peace to his mother?

Lucius's tears were nearly her undoing. She added her voice silently to his prayers as he begged over and over to be able to tell his mother of his conversion. It slowly began to sink into her fogged mind that he truly meant what he was saying.

They heard the front door open and Claudius returned with the physician. Lucius laid his mother back onto the bed, stepping back so that the physician could take over. He studied Leah for several minutes before he stood back and shook his head.

"There's nothing more I can do for her."

Lucius looked in disquiet from the physician to his mother, shaking his head. "No, there has to be something you can do!"

"Listen to her breathing. Her lungs are filling up with blood."

The sound Lucius made was like a wounded animal. He dropped to the bed, taking his mother in his arms again and laying his cheek against hers. Tears rained down his face in an unceasing river. Anna's own face was drenched, as well.

The physician took his leave unnoticed. Anna sat down beside Lucius and placed an arm around his shoulders. She didn't know what else to do.

Leah gasped suddenly, her eyes opening wide although the paralyzed side of her face drooped more than usual. She slowly raised a trembling hand and laid it against Lucius's cheek.

Lucius lifted his head, searching her face anxiously. "Mother?"

"Lucius." Her voice was little more than a breathy whisper, but it brought a wide smile to Lucius's face.

"Thank You, Elohim! Oh, praise You, Lord!"

"Lucius?"

"It's all right now, Mother," he told her softly, urgently. "I have accepted Jesus as my Lord and General Atticus baptized me just hours ago."

Peace settled down on Leah's twisted features. She was losing her fight to live but she hung on valiantly. "Anna?"

"I'm here, Leah."

Anna took Leah's hand and laid it against her own cheek. Leah tried to smile but the paralysis had become too severe. Anna caught Lucius's empathetic look and knew that they were sharing the same pain.

Leah's breathing became more shallow. She struggled to form just one word. "Marry!"

Lucius gently brushed the hair back from her face, kissing her on the cheek. "Yes, Mother. We are going to get married."

Leah tried to suck in a deep breath but failed. Her eyes widened then fluttered closed, her breath rushed out in a long exhale and she was gone. Moaning, Lucius buried his face against her neck.

Lucius sprinkled flowers from the garden onto the ivory bed whereon his mother lay. She was dressed in a white tunic and palla. Free from pain, her face was relaxed, at peace.

This day was much different from the day he had cremated his father. On that day, he had felt little but remorse that he and his father had never been able to have the kind of relationship that Petronius and his sons had. And unlike that day, today wave upon wave of pain numbed him to the point that he could hardly function.

Anna came next to him and took his hand in hers. He looked down into her swimming brown eyes and knew she was feeling the same. He gently squeezed her hand. He didn't know what he would have done these past few days if it hadn't been for her. His conversion to the Way had unlocked that portion of her heart that she had held away from him, and she had been the rock that he had leaned on.

Releasing all of his pent-up anger and hatred had been easier than he had anticipated. It was clear now that what Anna had told him was true. Everything works for the good of those who love the Lord. Elohim had planned his life out from the beginning. He still wasn't certain what that purpose was, but he knew that it included Anna.

Unlike his father's funeral, at Anna's assertion, he had chosen something simpler for his mother. The elaborate *justa facere,* or last honors, of the wealthy in Rome was something his mother would not have approved of. And instead of cremation, he had remembered his mother's request to be buried. Since burial inside the city was forbidden, he was willing to purchase land outside the city for that purpose, but the Christians had offered him an alternative. Later tonight he would be taking his mother to her final resting place outside the city in the labyrinth of catacombs used by the Christians. To rest among other believers—his mother would like that.

He needed no paid mourners for his mother. The atrium was filled to overflowing with people in white, weeping. The friendship that had been denied to his mother in Jerusalem had blossomed here in Rome, mainly due to her loving and generous heart.

General Atticus came and stood beside him. "She is with the Lord now, Lucius. The time for grieving is past. She would want you to go on with your life."

Soldier to soldier, Lucius understood what he meant. Life went on. But it was going to be a much lonelier place without his mother. Even with Anna by his side, it was going to take some time for the pain to recede.

When it was finally time to move the litter, Lucius took Anna's hand and, together, they followed behind the bier. This was no ordinary funeral procession. There was no long line of mourners. The catacombs were a well-kept secret and the mourners would join them there. What was his life going to be like now? Should he stay in Rome or take Anna and go to someplace like Alexandria in Egypt?

"I love you."

Anna's soft voice interrupted his thoughts, washing over him, filling his heart and reducing the pain. He glanced down at her and tried to smile.

"I love you, too, *carissima*."

"I am here for you."

Her brown eyes glowed with her love for him, and all his doubts were suddenly put to rest. His smile grew. As long as they were together, he could face anything.

They walked the rest of the way in silence, content to be in each other's presence, and content with the fact that his mother had gone before them to a better place and they would one day join her.

Epilogue

The chill of the cool air blowing down from the open roof of the atrium was offset by the warmth of the hypocaust heating system beneath the marble floor. Winter had come to Rome.

Lucius looked around him at the crowd of people who had come to see Anna and him exchange marriage vows. The warmth of dozens of human bodies added to the ambient air temperature. Many had been invited and many had come.

His heart swelled with gratitude for those who had become his friends over the last month. The emptiness of a home without his mother had been lessened by the many people who had come to him to tell him what his mother had done for them. And all without his having known. A twinge of pain twisted his heart. How he wished that he had been a part of that time in her life.

Lucius glanced across the room at his soon-to-be bride and thought, not for the first time, that she was the most beautiful woman in the world. How had he ever considered her plain? Knowing she was loved had given her a glow that radiated out to anyone in her vicinity.

She looked up and caught his glance and her face colored brightly although she didn't look away. Her luminous brown eyes were filled with a joy that humbled him when he realized that it was because of him. He would spend the rest of his life trying to keep that look in her eyes.

The white wool tunic she had chosen as her wedding garment set off the dark color of her skin, and her long brown hair hung in a lustrous sheen down her back. His fingers itched to run through it, but it was her pomegranate-red lips that caught and held his attention. This wedding couldn't happen soon enough for him.

General Atticus motioned for everyone to enter the peristyle. The eating tables and reclining couches had been removed to accommodate the large group of people that had gathered.

Anna joined Lucius to stand before the general and the room grew silent.

General Atticus bowed his head to ask a blessing on their union. Both Lucius and Anna had refused to make their vows before the priests of heathen gods, but as the general was a brother in the Lord, they had decided that this was what Christ would approve of. He prayed as one familiar with the act, one who spoke to a friend. Yet, the timbre of voice left no doubt of the reverence and respect for the Great I AM.

The general then took a golden cord and loosely joined Anna and Lucius at the wrists.

"Lucius and Anna, God instituted marriage because He saw that it was not good for man to be alone. A cord of one strand is easily broken, as is a cord of two. But when three strands are woven together, they are impossible to break."

Atticus then placed a hand on each of their shoulders.

"Lucius, will you promise to love Anna just as Christ loved the church? To be willing to die for her? To forsake all others and cleave only to her?"

The love glowing in Anna's eyes quickened his heart rate until he thought it would surely burst from his chest. "I pledge to do so."

"And will you, Anna, promise to love Lucius and submit to him in all things as the body does to Christ?"

A slow smile curled her lips. "I pledge to do so."

Lucius felt as though if he continued to stare into her eyes, he would sink into oblivion. It was hard to keep his mind on what they were doing when all he wanted to do was take Anna into his arms.

Atticus cleared his throat, grinning wryly when he caught Lucius's look.

"Then let me remind you of the words of the great Apostle Paul. 'Love is patient, love is kind. It does not envy, it does not boast, it is not proud. It is not rude, it is not self-seeking, it is not easily angered, it keeps no record of wrongs. Love does not delight in evil, but rejoices with the truth. It always protects, always trusts, always hopes, always perseveres. Love never fails.'"

Such love was daunting to think about. Lucius was learning that by himself, he could do nothing, but with Elohim, all things were possible.

Lucius took the ring he had had made especially for Anna. Lifting her left hand, he slid the ring onto her finger. "It is a Roman custom to wear a ring, an unending circle that symbolizes that our love is eternal, without end." He grasped both of her hands with his, sliding his fingers between hers and squeezing gently. "This is the love I pledge to you."

Anna had to swallow hard to remove the lump that had formed in her throat. She stared into Lucius's gleaming gray eyes, unable to speak for the moment. The love reaching out to her was something she had never expected to receive in her life, making it all the more precious.

The words of King Solomon came back to her now. "Hope deferred makes the heart sick, but a longing fulfilled is a tree of life."

She would never understand why Lucius had chosen her. Only Elohim could have so blessed her life.

Knowing the Roman custom, Anna was prepared. Taking the ring she had been given by Leah, she placed it on Lucius's hand. Surprised, he lifted a brow in inquiry.

"It belonged to your father." She awaited his response with bated breath. Would he refuse it? She wouldn't blame him if he did, but she hoped that he would understand that she had given it to him as a gift from his mother as well as herself.

Tears welled in his eyes as he stared at the ring, but he pressed his lips tightly together to ward them off. He looked at her when he had himself under control.

"Thank you, *carissima*."

He bent to kiss her, and she felt the warmth of it from head to toe. His kiss lingered, growing bolder until a cough and a few embarrassed chuckles forced them apart.

Atticus again placed a hand on each of their shoulders. "What God has joined together, let no man separate."

A series of amens arose from the crowd. Anna took the golden cord and laid it aside to be added to her treasure box. She then faced the room of well-wishers with her husband by her side. The crowd surged around them, offering them blessings of goodwill.

Was it possible to feel more joy than she did at this moment? She hoped and prayed that she could be the kind of wife Lucius needed.

Lucius motioned to the tables loaded with food set up

along the edges of the room. "My friends, come and share our wedding feast."

He stood looking about the room solemnly. Intuitively, she knew what he was thinking. Leah had been in this house only a short time yet she had left her mark everywhere.

"She was right, you know," he stated, looking down at her. "It was Elohim that brought us together."

She agreed. All the days of abuse, all the days of feeling inferior, had been worth it. She wouldn't change a thing about her past because it had molded her into the woman that he had fallen in love with, a woman of God.

Lucius took her hand and together, they joined the others. She didn't know what the future might hold, but she knew Who held the future.

She had once thought that she was cursed by Elohim, but had found living water that had quenched her thirst for love.

She had once thought that she was unlovable, destined to lead a lonely life, but Elohim had other, greater plans for her life.

Yes, with God, all things are possible.

* * * * *

REQUEST YOUR FREE BOOKS!

2 FREE CHRISTIAN NOVELS
PLUS 2
FREE
MYSTERY GIFTS

HEARTSONG

PRESENTS

YES! Please send me 2 Free Heartsong Presents novels and my 2 FREE mystery gifts (gifts are worth about $10). After receiving them, if I don't wish to receive any more books I can return the shipping statement marked "cancel." If I don't cancel, I will receive 4 brand-new novels every month and be billed just $4.24 per book in the U.S. and $5.24 per book in Canada. That's a savings of at least 20% off the cover price. It's quite a bargain! Shipping and handling is just 50¢ per book in the U.S. and 75¢ per book in Canada.* I understand that accepting the 2 free books and gifts places me under no obligation to buy anything. I can always return a shipment and cancel at any time. Even if I never buy another book, the two free books and gifts are mine to keep forever.

159/359 HDN FVYK

Name	(PLEASE PRINT)	
Address		Apt. #
City	State	Zip

Signature (if under 18, a parent or guardian must sign)

Mail to the Harlequin® Reader Service:
IN U.S.A.: P.O. Box 1867, Buffalo, NY 14240-1867

* Terms and prices subject to change without notice. Prices do not include applicable taxes. Sales tax applicable in N.Y. This offer is limited to one order per household. Not valid for current subscribers to Heartsong Presents books. All orders subject to credit approval. Credit or debit balances in a customer's account(s) may be offset by any other outstanding balance owed by or to the customer. Please allow 4 to 6 weeks for delivery. Offer available while quantities last. Offer valid only in the U.S.

Your Privacy—The Harlequin® Reader Service is committed to protecting your privacy. Our Privacy Policy is available online at www.ReaderService.com or upon request from the Harlequin Reader Service.
We make a portion of our mailing list available to reputable third parties that offer products we believe may interest you. If you prefer that we not exchange your name with third parties, or if you wish to clarify or modify your communication preferences, please visit us at www.ReaderService.com/consumerschoice or write to us at Harlequin Reader Service Preference Service, P.O. Box 9062, Buffalo, NY 14269. Include your complete name and address.

HSPDIR13R

REQUEST YOUR FREE BOOKS!

2 FREE INSPIRATIONAL NOVELS
PLUS 2
FREE
MYSTERY GIFTS

Love Inspired®

YES! Please send me 2 FREE Love Inspired® novels and my 2 FREE mystery gifts (gifts are worth about $10). After receiving them, if I don't wish to receive any more books, I can return the shipping statement marked "cancel." If I don't cancel, I will receive 6 brand-new novels every month and be billed just $4.74 per book in the U.S. or $5.24 per book in Canada. That's a savings of at least 21% off the cover price. It's quite a bargain! Shipping and handling is just 50¢ per book in the U.S. and 75¢ per book in Canada.* I understand that accepting the 2 free books and gifts places me under no obligation to buy anything. I can always return a shipment and cancel at any time. Even if I never buy another book, the two free books and gifts are mine to keep forever.

105/305 IDN F49N

Name	(PLEASE PRINT)	

Address		Apt. #

City	State/Prov.	Zip/Postal Code

Signature (if under 18, a parent or guardian must sign)

Mail to the Harlequin® Reader Service:
IN U.S.A.: P.O. Box 1867, Buffalo, NY 14240-1867
IN CANADA: P.O. Box 609, Fort Erie, Ontario L2A 5X3

**Are you a subscriber to Love Inspired books
and want to receive the larger-print edition?
Call 1-800-873-8635 or visit www.ReaderService.com.**

* Terms and prices subject to change without notice. Prices do not include applicable taxes. Sales tax applicable in N.Y. Canadian residents will be charged applicable taxes. Offer not valid in Quebec. This offer is limited to one order per household. Not valid for current subscribers to Love Inspired books. All orders subject to credit approval. Credit or debit balances in a customer's account(s) may be offset by any other outstanding balance owed by or to the customer. Please allow 4 to 6 weeks for delivery. Offer available while quantities last.

Your Privacy—The Harlequin® Reader Service is committed to protecting your privacy. Our Privacy Policy is available online at www.ReaderService.com or upon request from the Harlequin Reader Service.
We make a portion of our mailing list available to reputable third parties that offer products we believe may interest you. If you prefer that we not exchange your name with third parties, or if you wish to clarify or modify your communication preferences, please visit us at www.ReaderService.com/consumerschoice or write to us at Harlequin Reader Service Preference Service, P.O. Box 9062, Buffalo, NY 14269. Include your complete name and address.

LIDIR13R

LARGER-PRINT BOOKS!

**GET 2 FREE
LARGER-PRINT NOVELS
PLUS 2 FREE
MYSTERY GIFTS**

Love Inspired®

SUSPENSE
RIVETING INSPIRATIONAL ROMANCE

Larger-print novels are now available...

YES! Please send me 2 FREE LARGER-PRINT Love Inspired® Suspense novels and my 2 FREE mystery gifts (gifts are worth about $10). After receiving them, if I don't wish to receive any more books, I can return the shipping statement marked "cancel." If I don't cancel, I will receive 4 brand-new novels every month and be billed just $5.24 per book in the U.S. or $5.74 per book in Canada. That's a savings of at least 23% off the cover price. It's quite a bargain! Shipping and handling is just 50¢ per book in the U.S. and 75¢ per book in Canada.* I understand that accepting the 2 free books and gifts places me under no obligation to buy anything. I can always return a shipment and cancel at any time. Even if I never buy another book, the two free books and gifts are mine to keep forever.

110/310 IDN F5CC

Name	(PLEASE PRINT)

	Apt. #
Address	

City	State/Prov.	Zip/Postal Code

Signature (if under 18, a parent or guardian must sign)

Mail to the **Harlequin® Reader Service:**
IN U.S.A.: P.O. Box 1867, Buffalo, NY 14240-1867
IN CANADA: P.O. Box 609, Fort Erie, Ontario L2A 5X3

**Are you a current subscriber to Love Inspired Suspense books
and want to receive the larger-print edition?
Call 1-800-873-8635 or visit www.ReaderService.com.**

* Terms and prices subject to change without notice. Prices do not include applicable taxes. Sales tax applicable in N.Y. Canadian residents will be charged applicable taxes. Offer not valid in Quebec. This offer is limited to one order per household. Not valid for current subscribers to Love Inspired Suspense larger-print books. All orders subject to credit approval. Credit or debit balances in a customer's account(s) may be offset by any other outstanding balance owed by or to the customer. Please allow 4 to 6 weeks for delivery. Offer available while quantities last.

Your Privacy—The Harlequin® Reader Service is committed to protecting your privacy. Our Privacy Policy is available online at www.ReaderService.com or upon request from the Harlequin Reader Service.

We make a portion of our mailing list available to reputable third parties that offer products we believe may interest you. If you prefer that we not exchange your name with third parties, or if you wish to clarify or modify your communication preferences, please visit us at www.ReaderService.com/consumerchoice or write to us at Harlequin Reader Service Preference Service, P.O. Box 9062, Buffalo, NY 14269. Include your complete name and address.

LISLPDIR13R

When helicopter pilot Creed Carter finds an abandoned baby
on a church altar, he must convince foster parent
Haley Blanchard that she'll make a good mom—and a
good match.

WHISPER FALLS

Baby in His Arms

by Linda Goodnight

Former gunslinger Hunter Mitchell wants to start his life over with his newly discovered nine-year-old daughter—and his best chance at providing his daughter a stable home is a marriage of convenience to her beautiful and fiercely protective teacher.

Charity **HOUSE**

The Outlaw's Redemption

by

RENEE RYAN

Available July 2013.